Main   ATIONS
OF THE DREAD

Marcia Douglas

THE MARVELLOUS
EQUATIONS
OF THE DREAD
a novel in bass riddim

A NEW DIRECTIONS PAPERBOOK

First published by Peepal Tree Press in 2016.

AUTHOR'S NOTE: Whilst some of the characters in this novel share names with people who had real life existences, here they are figments of the imagination, and any resemblance to real life events or persons is purely coincidental.

Manufactured in the United States of America
New Directions Books are printed on acid-free paper
Published as a New Directions Paperbook Original (NDP1412) in 2018
Design by Erik Rieselbach

Library of Congress Cataloging-in-Publication Data
Names: Douglas, Marcia, 1961– author.
Title: The marvellous equations of the dread : a novel in bass riddim / Marcia Douglas.
Description: New York : New Directions Publishing, [2018]
Identifiers: LCCN 2017055365 | ISBN 9780811227865 (alk. paper) | ISBN 9780811227872 (ebook)
Subjects: GSAFD: Fantasy fiction.
Classification: LCC PS3554.O8274 M37 2018 | DDC 813/.54—dc23
LC record available at https://lccn.loc.gov/2017055365

10 9 8 7 6 5 4 3 2 1

New Directions books are published for James Laughlin
by New Directions Publishing Corporation
80 Eighth Avenue, New York 10011

For the healing of the nations

Look for me in the whirlwind.
— MARCUS GARVEY

CONTENTS

RE-MIX

Xaymaca, 1494: Taino Woman Studies the Future

A woman stands and looks out to sea. There are three ships on the horizon—they do not surprise her. She has seen them in dreams many times before: the white man on deck with his big feet and long boots, his hair the colour of stringy papaya. He thinks he has come to take her Xaymaca, this land of wood and sweet riverwater, but this island is stubborn and will not be moved. The woman has already seen that end from the beginning.

Far-far in the distance, past the ships and the memories of ships, she sees figures dancing on the water to the music of a man uprising on the waves, revolution on his cheekbones, fantastic dreadfullness in his hair, a lion roaring on his finger. Listen, children, to what he cries.

VERSION

LEENAH

There is a bass-line that pulsates along the faults of this island, from the Blue Mountains to Santa Cruz, from Plantain Garden to Rio Minho; then travelling the coast, troubling the waters. They say each year the blue-green sea rises higher, pulled by the music of the people. Bass riddim moves underground and the sea lurches, dragging flotsam, broken shells, and ground hipbones. "Walk on the sand with reverence, hear?" These are the words I say to Anjahla. For the bones of our kin are in the waters—the grainy debris of slave cargo—fierce babymothers who jumped off the ships and into the ocean. They swallowed seawater but stayed strong inside.

"Are you a fierce babymother?" Anjahla asks.

"Yes," I say. "I am fierce."

"Mama," she says. And I like the way her lips make "m." "When I tell this story to my children, I am going to give it another ending. I am going to send the mothers a rescue ship to take them home."

"And what you will call your ship, Anjahla?"

She smiles and looks off in the distance. The horizon at Hellshire is hazy green, like the bit of seaweed caught in her hair. We are conscious of the warm sand under our feet. Egrets step deliberately.

The year we walked Hellshire, Anjahla was six, so I am jumping way ahead. Before that, there was Bob and Riva Man; and my mama and papa; and Winifred and Hector; and the Guinea woman, Murlina; and yes, the fierce babymothers; but even before them, there was the big silk cotton at Half Way Tree, and later, the young boy hanged from it for singing freedom. They say he died with a word at the tip of his tongue; and even three hundred years later, is restless to remember it. He is the reason—centuries after his dancing feet, and a clock tower erected in place of the tree—that the hands of the clock always told the wrong time. The dead can be agitated by unfinished business that way. And they say, too, that Bob has unfinished spirit things here; our underground bass is the riddim he'll ride on his return. Did Taino sister see that far? For there is something still—

RASTAMAN

[Cedars of Lebanon Hospital; May 11, 1981]

Zion ship a come-o!

LEENAH

Of Lions and Pigs and Sorrow Mango [Babylon, May 11, 1981]

On the day Bob Marley dies, the two stone lions in front of the New York Public Library roar. I&I know because I&I dream it—a roar vibrating my body as I walk up the steps. There are little bells on my sandals, my locs swinging against my back. Just when I shift my bag from one shoulder to the other, something ignites right at my tail bone, the sensation increasing to a roaring current, Rastaman vibration travelling my spine to the top of my head. As the roar leaves my body, I sneeze and look behind me, but no one is there and the lions at the curb are still stone. Later, I learn the news of Bob's passing from television.

I met Bob years ago in the street in London. He was walking down the road, his mane uprising, and he asked me where in this raasclaat place he could find a coconut water. I was glad that even in the nippy March air, bundled up with my coat and gloves on, I looked like the kinda yard woman who might know a coconut watering hole. Still, I thought his question funny and I said, "No coconut trees here, mate." He laughed and I liked the way he threw back his head and let his teeth scrape the air. I took him to the little West Indian pub on the corner where I worked and he sat by the window and drained a glass of orange juice and said, "Rasta-fari." He leaned back into his chair as if he owned it, as if he had owned every chair he had ever sat on, as if he owned the whole earth. He said he needed to know where to find the sufferahs, the people; he had come for the sufferahs. Then all of a sudden he stopped, his eyes absorbing me like scripture. When he finally spoke, he said, "Why yu never tell me yu deaf?" I knew he had not realized.

16

"Reading your lips is like eating wild guava," I said.

There was mischief in his eyes.

"Yu like wild guava?"

"Can a deaf girl know Jah?"

He smiled then and put my hand against his chest. When he sang, *No cry,* I closed my eyes and felt his voice on my palm. It was the most irie gift anyone had ever give me.

That was when I began to know him—the misbehaving hair in his eyebrow, the cheekbones which could balance an egg or a flame or a revolution, his slim hands, the tinge of fire under his skin, the roar-blue of his shirt like the colour of the Caribbean in a particular herb light. It was because of Bob that I began to grow my locs again—the dreads that Sunday teacher in Jamaica cut off when I was twelve. Teacher threw them in the bin and set them afire. "Rasta filthiness," she said. I was so shame. The whole street knew—the smell of my hair carried like news on the breeze. For the next eleven years the smell of burnt hair kept wafting back to me—on my bedclothes, in my school bag, from half-open drawers—and always unexpected as violence. Then Bob sang that day in the corner pub, and something else came back: Mama washing my hair in the river, oiling and twisting it as we sat on a rock in the sun. And her voice, *Jah live,* before she died. I had forgotten those words. I had even forgotten Mama's name, Vaughn. Her name was Vaughn. Violence will do that to you. Make you forget your mother's name. Perhaps I grew my dreads back to remember myself. The hair was stubborn at first, but soon grew restless, reaching downward toward tree roots and underground water, hunting for Mama and Papa, and Winnie and Grandpa Hector. Mama always said her dreads were transmitters— to the ancestors, to Jah—and mine became life-vines to Bob as well.

And so on this day in 1981, the 11th of May when Bob dies, this is how I&I immediately recognize the roar going up my spine and the whoosh and the wind and the power of his leaving. And I send him Jah-speed.

The next week, the island is in the midst of an eleven-day weeping. A friend sells his nine pigs—two sows, a boar and six piglets—

for understanding the uncleanliness of pork to Rasta, he wants to honour Bob, and feels the only way to do so is to cleanse his yard of abomination. He changes his name to Ras Redemption and takes to singing in his sleep, funny little off-key tunes punctuated by *selah, selah*. It is also the only year his mango tree does not bear.

On the eleventh day, people line the streets from Kingston to Nine Mile to pay respect—breddren and sistren, youth watching from the top branches of trees, schoolchildren, madmen, preachers, murderers, market women, babymothers, thieves, shopkeepers, teachers, gangsters, politrickans, bus drivers, the sufferahs and the downpressers, the wicked and the I-nointed; and for fifty-five miles, a wave of grief passes through us, moving like a heat from one person to the other; and on this day, for the momentary passing of Bob's funeral motorcade, there is one sorrow.

DUB-SIDE CHANTING

Track 12.0: Bob Marley and the Lion of Judah Meet

And at the end of the fifty-five mile weeping, the angel of Jah blows the fourth trumpet and the Book of Zion is opened. For eleven days since his last breath, the prophet-Marley has travelled a wind swirling with sea salt, fire dust, bay rum, and the molasses scent of ancestors, all the while the wailing of the woman-Rita pressing him on like a conqueror—straight to the right hand of Jah.

He lands on his feet, blinks in the star-apple light, sees a house with a kerosene lamp in the window, an old man outside peeling sugar cane, and he knows right away he has seen this place before—in a half-silence while smoking a spliff, at the bottom of a river in a dream. This time though, there is sense of arrival: a sign— "STUDIO D: THE DUB-SIDE"—is propped against a nutmeg tree; a dog barks from behind the house. The eleven-day journey through soul debris has parched prophet-Marley's throat and the old man, higherstanding, dips his cup in a water barrel, and waits.

Soon as Marley steps forward, the dog—a little Chihuahua—runs into the yard, almost knocks the cup from the old man's hand. The nutmeg tree leans to one side and the ground hums like a spinning record. Marley reaches for the cup, the taste, at first, as ordinary as St. Ann rain; but then—give-thanks-and-praise—the quench opens his Rastafareye, and all things are made clear: the Most High, His Imperial Majesty, Haile Selassie I of Ethiopia, the Conquering Lion of the Tribe of Judah, the King of Kings, Elect of God, is revealed before him— the old man in the torn shirt eating sugar cane.

And so it is the prophet and the Judah-lion stand at the redgreengold sign. Both small in stature, they meet eye-to-eye, the lion long-time stripped of his medallions, epaulettes and custom-made shoes; and Marley, all bald-head now—his locs uprooted by cancer, even the dread wig in which he was buried, left in the coffin, unable to traverse the space between Nine Mile and Jahliverance. The Judah-lion is the first to smile; he shows a row of missing teeth, his dentures samewise left behind, buried deep in the faeces his dead body was thrown in; the canines he depended on, now in the sewer under Colonel Mengistu's toilet, incapable under such weight to make the dread journey. For such are the mysteries of the Dub-side: Rasta-man without locs, lion without teeth.

In Babylon, Marley had hung a picture of His Imperial Majesty above his bed—H.I.M. regal and never-smiling. He smoked holy herb beneath that picture and made love there and wrote songs; he prophesied in season and out of season; called to pretty women outside the window; laughed and reasoned and dreamed dreams and awakened to the sirens in the street; traced downpressors, and longed for the taste of honey and pineapple—H.I.M. always watching sideways and serious. Much respect. Now the Judah-lion's toothless smile is absent of worry or botheration, and Marley, standing there face-to-face with the Almighty, feels the urge to sing, his voice a seven-chambered instrument filling the yard, redgreengold fire in the sound.

The Judah-lion listens, his eyes moist. He puts his hand on Marley's shoulder. "Whothe son are you?" His words, spoken without teeth, are sea foam.

The question stirs remembrance in Marley of the ring once worn by His Majesty-self—black onyx with a lion engraved in gold—which would prove he is a son of the Most High. He had guarded it from thieves and lovers, fire and water, and now, standing before Selassie-I, he feels for it on his middle finger, eager to establish that he is indeed a son of the Judah Lion, that he has fought a good fight and has been a careful steward.

He takes off the ring and puts it in His Majesty's palm. H.I.M. holds it to the light, contemplates a while, a little smile on his face. "My ring is in replica all over the streeths of Addis Ababa," he says, then drops it in a tin of cane trash. "This is just another one."

*

Somewhere down in Babylon, a breadfruit falls with a loud clap on a zinc roof. Tribulation. Marley tries to read His Majesty's face, but he still smiles. "Someone has tricked you," his eyes say. The prophet looks back at the place where he landed. Under the nutmeg tree a fog rises up like herb smoke, and the way back to Babylon has vanished.

HERE-SO; HALF WAY TREE

The Fall-down Angel of Hope Road

Back in Babylon where the weeping has subsided, it is raining and a radio at a bus stop on Hope Road plays a Marley tune as a fall-down angel taps foot to the one-drop beat. Every town has them—bredren and sistren who wander the streets, turn over garbage bins, point in your face and cry, "Babylon!" Some people call them mad, some people call them poets, some people call them fall-down angels.

The fall-down of Hope Road is afraid of no one. He is known to pull his ratchet knife out his back pocket and stare-down anyone from Governor General to bad dog. Sitting at this bus stop and then that one, he plays fool to catch wise and knows everybody's business. To this day, if people want to know the real Jamaica, they ask a fallen angel and if they want to know Bob's business, they ask the fall-down on Hope Road.

And so it is, back in Babylon at the intersection of Half Way Tree and Hope, Fall-down smiles a little smile as he imagines the Prophet on the Dub-side, his cancer-foot healed, and even the criss-cross lines which once marked his palms all disappeared, the skin a new parchment. A schoolboy shelters from rain beside the fall-down, and sings along with the radio, from time to time strumming an imaginary guitar.

"Zion," the fall-down whispers to no one in particular. His head is tied around and around with a red cloth and little brass Africas dangle from his ears.

"What about Zion, Fall-down?" the boy asks, for all the schoolchildren know the mad angel and mock him.

"Robert Nesta Marley must find where Zion is."

"Tell me about Bob," the boy says, as Fall-down reaches out and cups his hand to taste the rain.

"Few gateways to Zion, but Bob will find one of them."

"How you know, Mad-Ras?"

Fall-down does not answer. Every now and then there is a soft chime, and the boy is uncertain whether the clink-clink comes from the radio or from the little brass Africas.

"I bet you, not a raas ting go so," he says.

The rain is falling harder and a huddle of birds cuss over a piece of stale bread.

"There was a time when a boy would not talk to an angel like that."

"Tell me about Zion," says the boy, strumming guitar. "Where it is, Fall-down?"

"Somewhere special."

"But how you get there? You have to dead like Bob?"

There is another clink-clink, and a man's voice on the radio cries, "Bloodfiah!" For a while Fall-down does not answer. His eyes are far away, past the rain and the backed-up traffic, past the fence across the street and the birds on the cable wires.

"No, you don't have to dead to get there."

"Take me to Zion then," the boy says. "Get me outta this raas place."

Fruit flies circle his head, following him like specks in orbit. Fall-down taps his staff.

"Every now and then, somebody find it without looking," he says.

The boy is there the next afternoon with his school bag and holey shoes. All night he has searched in his dream for Zion, chopping his way through a thicket of bamboo, guango trees and long john-crow vines. He sits now on an overturned bucket by the bus stop, listening to the clink-clink of Fall-down's earrings, missing his bus then waiting for the next one and the one after that.

"Tell me again bout Zion, the place you say Bob must reach," he says.

It is Friday and the city is ablaze with heat and vice.

"*Awake, Zion, awake!*" Fall-down sings.

"Shut up," the boy says. "People can't even talk serious with you."

"Since when you take me serious, anyway?"

The boy sucks on a tamarind ball and spits out the seed.

"Alright, respect."

"Riddle me this; riddle me that. Guess me this riddle and per-haps not: My mother have many mansions and all of them have a different gate."

"So is more than one place?"

"No, is *one* place."

The boy looks confused.

"The arithmetics of Zion, youth-man! Maths like that no teach inna school."

The boy throws a stone at a bird in the lignum vitae tree behind him. The bird takes off, following the direction of traffic.

Another bus begins to pull away from the curb and Fall-down watches as a woman runs to catch it, the muskwhiff of her passing filling the air.

DUB-SIDE CHANTING

Track 13.0: Under the Nutmeg Tree

The holy herb fills the yard, swirls around the feet of Marley and His Imperial Majesty, so that soon the two stand in a river of smoke. Marley bends down, fans the air, anxious to peer back into Babylon to find where the true ring might be.

"Do not look back," H.I.M. says, and the smoke rises higher, touches their knees. "Since I have been here, I have witnessed it time and time again. Those who look back thlip and fall down, and never come back, and anyway, you do not want to return to 56 Hope Road, falling backwards like a fool."

And who is Marley to defy the Almighty? Down in Babylon, there are wars and rumours of wars. Marley feels the rumbling under his feet—gunshots and backfighting and all manner of politricks and wickedness and spoilation of the earth—a youth running across the street at Molynes Road, shot in the head; a politician's girlfriend locked in a freezer, poisoned water; stillborn infants; a stick rammed up a goat's ass; a man's slit throat.

As a sign between himself and Jah, he had been given the ring for the healing of the nation, and now for all his trials and sufferation, he has lost it. Marley looks back at the leaning tree, "STUDIO D" all covered in smoke. Somewhere in the distance there is a faint clink-clink, and he moves toward the sound.

"Wait."

H.I.M. speaks with a quiet assurance, holds up his hands like two tablets of stone. The last in a succession of 225 kings traced back through bloodfire to King Solomon and his court, H.I.M. lifts his voice and Rastafari listens. The indigo sky casts a bluish tinge on his palms, and as he speaks the smoke rises higher, covers his wrists and his slender fingertips.

"This work is not for you alone. Others will come afther," H.I.M. says, and his face disappears in the haze.

HERE-SO; HALF WAY TREE

Angel Is Fallen, Is Fallen

"Zion and angelshit to raas," the boy says, "so whose angel you was?"

"One time I had a girl right here in Kingston. She sold newspapers and box drink on the street, and I used to follow her so boys like you wouldn't touch her up."

"You too lie!"

The little brass Africas go clink-clink, but Fall-down does not answer.

"Mad man!" says the boy and begins to play his make-believe guitar.

The radio stops mid-note—out of batteries—and Fall-down puts it in the satchel with his shoe brush, bottle of kananga water and ledger book of happen-tings.

"I don't believe in no angels," the boy says, "I deal inna gunfire!" and he shoots out his arm like a machine gun.

After a while Fall-down says, all quiet, "I used to be an angel in King Solomon's court."

The boy rolls his eyes and looks away. He can see his bus coming and begins to leave.

"You like sexy girls?" Fall-down pulls at the boy's sleeve. "I used to be the angel who watched over King Solomon when he made love to his concubines."

He throws a coin in the air and catches it. It lands on Marcus Garvey's head.

"And I bet you never know that I was there when His Imperial Majesty of Ethiopia, the Elect of God, made love to the Empress while the lions watched?"

A girl in tight jeans and long plaits comes and stands at the bus stop. She opens a book with a gilded map of Jamaica on front.

"In the end, I fall from grace because I slept with a pretty woman." He sighs and watches the traffic. "An angel should not commit such acts with humans, you know. Not even in their dreams."

The bus is at the corner; the boy hesitates again then hops inside; this time the clink-clink he hears comes from the little Africas in syncopation with the dawta's silver bangles. Her gilded map catches the sun.

"Come back tomorrow, you hear?" Fall-down calls. "I go tell you how to love a girl."

LEENAH

London, 1977: The Language of Zion

Bob came back to the pub quite unexpectedly one afternoon—
searching for fresh orange juice. He held his head back and drained
the cup clean, then asked for another one.

"Yu want to know my vice?" he said. "Woman is my vice."

I acted as though I had not understood him, but as I watched
his Adam apple bob up and down, I had a sudden need to touch it.

"Yu too overripe," I said, and the apple throbbed under my finger. There was mischief in his eyes again.

He wanted to write me a song, he said, and he pulled the felt pen
from behind my ear, and wrote around and around on a paper cup,
tapping out beats on the wood counter. When he finished, he sang
it right then and there with my hand over his apple, taking it all in.

He left, still singing, the paper cup twirling on his forefinger, his
lion head held high in the cold rain. *Dawta of Zion, Jah-Jah Zion calling
come.* For a long time, I wondered whether the song would make
it to the radio; I don't think it did. But in my silence, the words
lived and my locs grew, and I hungered for the company of lions.

Sometimes I made him a juice of banana, pineapple and mango
from the West Indian market. Business was slow and we spoke in
between customers. I had fashioned a Rasta sign language, funny
I&I-taught motions which he caught onto quickly, me the mel-
ody and he the dub root bass. We spoke the same language, me
and Bob. My hands moved like music. Like reggae to a one-drop
beat. I had taken the signs they taught at deaf evening school and
transformed them into full-joy and roots drink/Almighty Jah and
revelation and rice/run-down and shad and mackerel and green

banana and dumpling/and apprecilove and compellance and/red green and gold and give thanks and praise/remembrance of livication; for who is there to teach the true sign for Zion? You must she-magine it yourself.

"Our lives are crossed," I said to Bob one day, "like two roads which meet at a junction," and I lay my arms one over the other.

"Bloodclaat," is all he said, and blew a circle of smoke in the air.

But I understood. He thought I meant I had fallen in love with him. He was used to that. One day I saw him walk by with a woman with long wavy hair. He turned and smiled and gave me a peace sign, and the woman turned and smiled too, confident in the stride of her brown legs, but holding Bob's hand a little tighter.

I filled his glass again.

"Mind you become vain," I said.

"What?"

"Don't get it in your head that every nice-girl loves you."

He looked at me, stirring his drink, pondering my words.

"Woman to rise up inna love, no fall," he said.

A draft of air came in as a man opened the door and sat at the other end of the counter.

"Rising or falling, not every pretty woman wants you, you know. And anyway," I said, "we are joined together in the house of Zion, not love."

But I did love him, though not in the falling down way he thought. Deaf-life had made me a standing tree. I stood now like a Royal Poinciana on the other side of the counter. I had my pride and would not let his "bloodclaat" pass without comment, even if he flashed me his country boy smile. A chilly gust blew from a cracked window and I turned and served a glass of beer to the man who had just come in.

When I returned, Bob was leaning back in his chair, studying me with his river-bottom eyes.

"Talk Rasta with your hands. I-man understand Rasta."

I softened a little then. My hands made I&I and opened like a pod; the insides spilled with black seeds.

The man at the other end drank his beer and watched. I closed my eyes and leaned across the counter, close to Bob's ear.

"I&I was not always a deaf girl in London, you know. The sound I&I remember most of all is the dogs in Kingston barking late at night. There was also a lizard which lived behind the photo of my mother on the bedroom wall; I remember its croaking, though I can't remember my mother's voice. She died when I was twelve years old; she had give me one of her locs and I lost it. Losing the loc was like losing the key to Zion gate.

But the last sound I heard before I turn deaf-girl was you, on a jukebox. Someone was playing it in a bar across the street. You were singing—"

"*Duppy Conqueror*," he said.

He was right. That was the song. And in that instant, I could tell he was stunned at his words, the consonance we shared.

"You want to know my vice?" I say.

HERE-SO; HALF WAY TREE

The Desires of the Flesh

Fall-down stands and draws himself up to his full height. He is a tall man and the red cloth which wraps his head makes him appear even taller. He stretches up and raises both arms as if waiting for flight.

"I specialize in the desires of the flesh," he says.

The boy is suddenly interested. He stops biting his nails and looks up. Fall-down taps him on the head.

"How old you is?"

"Twelve, Ras."

"Then you old enough to appreciate my line of work."

"Yes?"

"I am not the angel who catch babies when them drop or save planes from crash, you know. No, not me. I am the angel who help a man perform! And make sure a woman satisfy!"

The boy begins to giggle.

"Like Cupid?"

"Nah. Cupid specialize inna love. I specialize inna eros. Two different thing."

"Liard!" the boy says, laughing.

"Stay there laugh. You think Solomon coulda manage so much concubine without help?" Fall-down's face is serious, a profane scripture.

"And look the one, Bob. How much woman him did go through?"

At this, the woman selling box drinks and peanuts next to the bus stop turns around.

"Listen, I could tell you some tings about what happen inna that bed at No. 56, right there underneath Jah photograph."

"I know what you going say—you was Bob angel too," says the boy.

"But of course. How you think I reach Hope Road?"

The boy looks up at the sky as if looking for signs.

"When Bob was alive, him coulda get any woman him want. And is me show him how," Fall-down says.

He twirls his staff around on its end. It spins like a top before toppling into his hand.

"One time, I steal one of Bob's pretty woman, you know." His eyes are wistful. "Is sake a she me fall."

"So is Bob fire you!" says the woman, laughing.

But Fall-down is not listening. He is standing at the curb oblivious to the mayhem of horns and swerving cars, waiting for a Kingston breeze, waiting to take off.

"I entered her room through the back of her dream," he says. "I wish I coulda find that dawta again."

A big truck speeds by, splashing dirty water, soaking his shoes.

"But yu bamboo fallen down," says the woman, her belly shaking.

The brass Africas begin to jingle. Fall-down steps into the middle of the street. No one pays him much attention—the people are used to madmen and prophets and the fallen-from-grace. He raises his arms in the air, "Deliverance!"

Only the boy sees the strange little bird which darts on his shoulder, then takes off quick-quick flying across the city of zinc and concrete and mango trash.

"Tell me about Bob pretty woman!" he calls.

Track 7.0: The Transgression of Negus

She read about him in a book she had found in a dream. His name was Negus and he used to be King Solomon's angel; the angel who advised the king on how to seduce the Queen of Sheba. For in those days, it was written: "There is a place of desire, a tabernacle of Zion, only Negus can find." In her dream, she wanted to memorize the story line by line, but because it was late, the night almost gone, she saved her page with a croton leaf and closed the book. When she awoke, her pillow smelled of cinnamon, and underneath was a dragonfly with antennae long as guitar strings.

Next-night as she undressed in the dark, she recognized the silhouette of wings in the breadfruit tree. It was him, Negus, resting naked like a great insect, for he had travelled through falling stars and the bottoms of dreams and needed now to catch his breath. Her dress slipped to the floor, fallen-down bougainvillea, and she watched. When at last he climbed down from his perch and into her room, he was holding the book from the dream. No words passed between them, but she reached for it, the cover still warm from journey. And deep the book played a bass groove; and deep the groove grew a calabash; and deep the calabash was a stone; and deep the stone was a flame; and deep the flame breathed a mirror of secrets; and deep the mirror her nakedness reflected, ripe like Bombay mango.

The third night, he unfolded his wings—magnificent in their breadth and stitched from the feathers of 307 species of hummingbird—and teased her with one quill. The room filled immediately with little glistening things: nutmeg dust, yellow cornmeal, sea salt, shimmered sugar, sequin fish scales.

The fourth night he appeared at the window all blue-black from the moonshine; his eyes were transparent like bottle-glass and she saw straight through them to the other side where a lizard on a tree bark stretched its wet tongue. This time he brought naseberry and guava cheese; fed her paw-paw and coconut cream; filled her navel with honey and drank it like an elixir; traced a labyrinth on her belly with hibiscus pollen. She was ravenous and partook unashamed, for what did it matter? His palms had no lines and there was no past and no future, only pleasure.

Fifth night, the night of scent, and the cricket on the windowsill rubbed its legs together. Ras Angel's nostrils flared like celestial moths as he took her inside of himself in great drafts and little puffs, smelling her up and down, recording each scent—seventeen in all—on the parchment of his thigh. With each pore numbered and counted, for the first time she was known, her name written down.

The sixth night he oiled her scalp with wisdom weed soaked in rose-olive. Her alive locs moved like spirit fronds and she raised her arms to reveal little hairs humid as baby fern. When he pulled her clothes down below her belly, he found god-bush ready and impatient.

On the seventh night she waited by the open window. He arrived with a gush of Orion and carrying a guitar carved from cedar and set with cowries and polished stones, each dragonfly string tuned and tightened to the reverberation of longings. For again in the word it is written, "The archangel holds the seventh chord of desire." And at the end of that tuning, it was she, now, who called him with her eyes, bass root moving up through her woman chamber—chime of star apple, chime of blood, chime of purple, chime of sweet water, chime of heat, chime of passion-flower, chime of Zion—and she saw herself reflected ripe in her fever as the mirror increased the flame and the flame heated the stone and the stone desired the calabash and the calabash craved the bass and the bass trembled in the book and the book opened in the dream, and the angel said, Yes-I, Yes-I.

LEENAH

Beetle

And then there was the time I came across Bob standing by a lamp-post on Cheney Road. He was staring down the long pavement and the row of stuck-together-houses wondering where on Jah earth he had landed. It was cold and he was not dressed for the weather—he wore a denim shirt layered over a long-sleeved tee. When I called out his name, he looked relieved to see me. As he stepped off the curb, he sang a line from his song, *Dawta of Zion, Jah-Jah Zion Dawta Come*, fog wafting from his mouth.

"All the raasclaat house-them look the same to me," he said.

"Silly." I poked him in the ribs.

I helped him back to his little flat off Cheney. The place smelled of herb and orange rind. There was a picture of His Majesty on the wall. We sat by the window smoking and drinking Chinese green tea. He leaned back in his chair absorbing me in his usual way. H.I.M. watched from his place above the bed, wearing his crown of crowns; his velvet cloak looked uncomfortable. It had been almost three years since the reports of His Majesty's passing.

"The day the news came, I was folding clothes at the launderette; I saw it on the BBC," I said.

"Babylon Bomboclaat C." Bob pulled at his spliff and watched the smoke float up. "Jah can't dead. Jah always live. Look, even inna the rain him live. Facts. Facts is facts."

We both stared at the rain coming down sideways and drizzling against the window.

"I still think he died," I said.

"Rasta no deal with death."

"I mean his body died."

I nudged at a beetle on the windowsill with my spoon. It wouldn't move. We were quiet for a while, smoking. Bob blew a circle into the air.

"Sometime Peaches let me blow smoke on her pum-pum," he said.

I knew who Peaches was—the woman with the long wavy hair. She looked stylish and maybe famous. The kind of woman who looked good with a star like Bob.

"She like it?"

"Yeah-man."

I laughed and twirled my finger like smoke circles. He smiled mischievously. I knew what he wanted, but preferred the dance.

"Jah live," I said.

He leaned forward and brushed my lip with his finger and I smiled, but pulled away.

"You have someting to hide?"

"Like?"

"Every woman have a secret. Woman deal inna secrecy."

"Who are you to talk."

He passed the spliff back to me and the smoke filled my head. His eyes had little wheels in the middle of wheels.

"The Queen of Sheba came to Solomon with a cloven hoof," he said.

(For this island is full of secrets. And know, too, there are some which have never been found, for only the feet of the steadfast can find such, and even then, only if it happens to be a particular day of the year when the earth is tilted just-so and your mind is on something else like sweet-sop or overripe guava.

One day you are out searching for those guavas when your foot slips, finding an opening in the mountainside. You wonder how after all these years trodding this land and reasoning with it, you never knew this place. You hear the gurgle of a stream and make your way towards it, eager to drink. The water is sweet, tinged with rose-apple and you know right away this is no ordinary cave.

And now, because you have stirred the water and because on this particular day, the earth is tilted just-so, Riva-Mumma awakes from sleep, her scales jingling like coins. When she appears, you see that this Riva-Mumma don't shape like a picture-book mermaid; no. This Mumma wears a long skirt made of skin—a blue flesh grown down from the span of her waist, covering her legs and adorned with every precious riva-bottom thing. When Riva-Mumma dances, the skirt-of-skin—all a-shimmer with scales—ripples like a meeting of waters, revealing her ankles and twelve shell toes. Long-long dreads alive with water-moss, snails and little specks of sand grow all the way to her navel. The navel is closed-shut and barely visible, for she is now the last of her kind. From Taino to Dancehall, she knows the history of this island backwards and forwards, and can answer any question put to her. For, when all is said and done, this is why you are here, no true? After Riva-Mumma finish spin and spin, she steadies her head and laughs a water laugh, looks you in the eye, waiting for your question. You better have one ready or you will lose your chance.

"Riva-Mumma," you say, "Is it true a boy died with a word at the tip of his tongue?")

38

LEENAH

London, 1977: The Country in Her Voice

I noticed the ring one day as Bob tapped out a tune on the counter, the proud lion emblazoned in gold, unabashed in its glory.

"Sometimes is like lightning on my finger," he said, and he rubbed the ring against his chin, then made a fist and touched it to mine. I picked up the beat and signed, "Lion of Judah," my palms opening and clenching bass against my body.

He had received the ring only the week before, a gift from Haile Selassie's son, Prince Asfa Wossen. The prince explained that the ring—a family heirloom—had belonged to his father and that now, he wanted it to be worn by Bob. For Bob had shown honour to his father as only a faithful son can.

"Let me try it on," I said. "See if it burn me too."

But Bob became cross, "Is no joke ting this," and pulled away.

Later he said that even before he received the ring, he had seen it years before in a dream—a small man in uniform gave him a gold ring set with a black stone. The man rode into Bob's sleep on a horse, looking important and official. No words passed between them, but the horseman put the ring on his finger, then left. When Bob told me this story, I imagined the horse galloping, leaping through his dream and on through the dreams of all the ring's predecessors to King Solomon sleeping on a feather bed. I had read about King Solomon's ring once, how he tamed wolves with it. But this was not the real Ring of Solomon on Bob's finger, was it? I wanted to know more, but seeing the bushfire in Bob's eyes, decided to leave him alone. Something about the ring scared him. We both wanted to change the subject.

He asked for club soda, "I-man don't deal with strong drink,"

39

and watched as I put away glasses on a shelf. I could tell he wanted to say something and when I caught his reflection in the mirrored wall, he said, "Where inna Jamaica you grow?"

"Brown's Town and Kingston. I came here when I was fourteen," I said. And then a thought came to me and I said, "What country you hear in my voice?"

He said, "Kingston with likkle London, and a funny riddim underneath that wash up now and then like the sea."

I made a wavy motion with my fingers and thought of dead fish washed up on Hellshire Beach, frothy waves, an overcast Kingston sky eager to rain.

He looked out the window contemplating the clouds, put down his glass and said, "So how you end up inna this raas country?"

And I said, "I killed a girl, and had to take her place."

Because I couldn't tell it face to face, I turned my back and spoke to Bob's reflection in the mirror-wall. There was a parade outside and the pub was empty. Through the mirror, I could see Bob stroking his beard. When the words came, they flew quick as birds, circled the pub and swooped through the back window; I was glad I could not hear them—

I was standing at the bus stop at Crossroads when I saw my neighbour, Verle, and her grandmother across the street; her hair had been recently pressed and it was all shiny and she had a big smile on her face. I knew Verle's grandmother well because she used to be a Sunday school teacher in Uncle's church and it was she who came to cut off my locs after Mama died, and they sent me to Kingston. The whole time she cutting my hair she said, "Rasta nastiness, what kinda nastiness." Verle with a little smirk on her face, was poking at the fallen dreads with a stick. Her grandmother threw the locs away in the rubbish, set it on fire, then washed her hands with blue soap. That day when I saw them at Crossroads they were just coming back from the British Embassy; I knew it because all week Verle had been going on about her appointment for her visa and how she couldn't wait to get on the plane and kiss Jamaica goodbye to raas. So I couldn't help it—watching Verle cross the street, I imagined her in England drinking tea and eating sponge cake and wearing little white gloves and I had a bad thought and called her Queen Elizabitch. I said the words right out loud, Queen Elizabitch, and I wished her dead. So Verle and her grandmother were in the middle of the road, manoeuvering traffic, and I had just barely had that wicked thought when a minivan swung from around the corner and knocked Verle down. She bounced up into the air and landed on the sidewalk, her canvas shoes flying off, all the loose change and bubble gum and tampons in her shoulder bag scattered. Her grandmother's mouth went, Veeeerle! Jesusjesusjesusjesusjesus! I saw her mouth open and close like slow-motion movie. And in my fright, I couldn't breathe; I turned around and ran and ran and ran all the way home to Papine. I was late with the newspaper-cod-liver-oil-and-dragon-stout and expected a cussing, my uncle waiting with the strap; but instead, he sat on the couch reading a letter with a big smile on his face—he had heard from his sister in England, and she wanted to send for me, to "take her off your hands," she wrote, and right away I knew that there would be no pleasure in leaving, for everything had been shaken around, me to end up in London to rah, instead of Verle.

I stopped to catch my breath and Bob said, "Fear not." It was the first time I had told anyone about Verle. Outside clouds were gathering, but there was clapping and cheering at the passing parade. A marching band played and a man waved a Union Jack.

I watched Bob's lips in the mirror.

"Check this," he said. "When I-man was a youth, I could read the future. One time, I read a woman hand-middle and see that she wouldn't live. Soon after, she keel off her mule and dead." His voice quiet, he looked at his hand and opened and closed his fist, twirled the ring on his finger.

"Part of me did think is me cause it."

In the mirror his face lit up against a flash of lightning. He took a last swig of his drink.

"What made you come to this raas country?" I said.

"Politricks. Isms and skisms. Gunman—"

Outside there was thunder and it began to pour, a woman dashed in from the parade shouting, "Oh God!" half at the lightning and half at seeing Bob.

He lifted his right hand, "Rastafari," then left through the side door, disappearing in the rain. He was always disappearing in rain.

BACKGROUND SINGER SOUND SISTREN [SISTAH WILLA]

Track 4.0: The Youth-prophet, Robert Nesta Marley

For there is a rain in Jamaica that comes down like horses. Massa's horses, galloping three-hundred years to the ancestor standing at a split in the path, searching for the way to Zion-high. Every time old-time people hear that rain, they urge the ancestor on, knowing that her feet-them small, but quick.

For the hand of this island is criss-cross just like the ancestors' path, yes—Priestess Nanny and Bogle, and someone's Urselyn and Cyril and Ethel and David, and the youth with the word-at-his-tongue. And don't forget—the Nine Mile Marley boy, Nesta. That last one had it in him from the start to do spirit line of work; yes, he used to read hands and was good at it. But he hear a sound zing-zing from afar and the sound fill him, and he set his vision instead on the neck-strings of guitar. But look. Look how his guitar prophesy same like the writing on the left hand of Jah. Two paths; same prophet. Marley. Selah.

For it is written, even in those days—six years old—he had a look in his eyes that swim the bottoms of mossy waters, count and name every stone and swallow-down fish whole. Sweet Jah.

Hear this: it was horse-rain falling the day a woman saw Nesta under the grocery shop piazza—

LEENAH

Of Herstory

I&I knew this story. Or a version of it. Bob was that way. Plenty times when he was with me I had the feeling that all things connected, the smoke from our spliff all mingled together. Bob made me feel that way, and that was part of what I meant when I said, "Our lives are crossed." Watching Bob talk about the rain and the woman on the shop piazza with the criss-cross hand-middle, filled me with remembrance. Stories are that way. In little districts of Jamaica, they travel and reverb for generations.

"A boy took Eunice hand-middle and studied it like a will," is what people said. Whenever I think of this story, it plays out in my head with humming. And bongo drums. And rain. No words. The boy reads her hand-middle and sees her whole life. He looks at her with river-bottom eyes. Afterwards, she gives him a mint from her pocket, watches him put it in his mouth as he walks away. When he is out of sight, she opens both her palms, and lets the rain fall on the astonishment there. She dies the next week.

Each time my mother told that story, she got all quiet-and-meditation. Then she would take a broom and sweep the verandah from corner to corner.

I always wondered who the little boy was and where he went. And now, I realized. And remembered another story—about the boy and the Bobo Rasta, Riva Man, who used to sell us brooms. Riva Man was mute. People say that as a baby he hardly cried, and when he did it was fresh-wata tears. As he grew, he became a child of few words, then one day he stopped speaking altogether. They say that one day, not long after Eunice died, the Marley boy put his hand on top of Riva's own, and said, "Take this crosses from me," and that's how he gave Riva his second sight. Riva was a youth of about seventeen at the time; no one was surprised when he wrap his head and turn Bobo Rasta and start to make thatch brooms and roots drink, and travel and balm the murmur-heart of the island, parish to parish, reasoning to himself. Whatever future Riva saw when he read the hand of Jamaica, he did not speak it. What he did do was make Zion of whatever he found.

Every new-year, Mama bought a broom from Riva. By then, he was a grown man; he was like an uncle to me. I liked him because whenever he was around he made things feel peace-and-sanctify. I&I felt an immediate I-finity with him—his muteness and my deafness. Back then, I was one of the few who understood his silent-speak, the signs he had made to express himself. He would disappear for weeks sometimes, and then turn up with a bag of roots drink, his brooms on his shoulder; he'd spend the whole day on the verandah all smoky and dreamfull and far-away. In times of tribulation, it was his broom Mama would use to sweep herself to fullness.

One day she went inside to turn off the pot and Riva made his hands like a Coca-Cola bottle; he wanted me to know that her roundness was beautiful. He wrote the word "Empress" on his fore-arm with a piece of coal. I think my mother liked him too because he smiled a lot but was quiet, and therefore did not interfere. She was tired of interference. This was after Papa died and she liked the way his eyes watched her without being threatening. And he looked out for us too. By then Gran Winnie was dead as well, and it was just the two of us. People in the district did not like Rasta. They thought we were turning the island into backwardness. An evangelist was in the habit of visiting the yard, just standing there as if he had a god-given right, praying and rebuking us to dutty hell fire.

"Is where hell?" I asked Mama.

"You in it," she said.

She put an extra lock on the door and painted a sign: "No Word

Used Against This House Shall Prosper." Riva Man put up a red-green-&-gold flag on a bamboo pole, and then swept the place clean with great care and ceremony, cleansing it of every evil thing. We named the yard House of Zion. After that, my mother got a new reputation—obeah woman. Still, she wrapped her locs pretty in a piece of yellow cloth and stepped out into the road like the empress that she was. I practiced to hold my neck high like hers, though there were always eyes watching from behind a fence, words mumbled, "Dutty gal," under the breath.

The last time I saw Riva Man was in 1966 when my mother died. All my life I&I have wanted to find him since.

HERE-SO; HALF WAY TREE

Shoe Brush
[Found Sound]

For a whole week, Fall-down does not see the boy. Then he returns one day wearing his dusty back-pack and worn shoes and with a look on his face of a warrior come back from war. He stands at the bus stop, his shoulder against the zinc fence. A police car, siren blaring, weaves its way through traffic, headed toward Crossroads. Schoolchildren and vendors of every made-in-china thing fill the sidewalks.

"Babylon!" Fall-down calls after the police car. The boy, lost in thought, watches a dead roach carried by an army of ants. The police car disappears around the corner and Fall-down picks up his staff. It is one he has carved himself—a snake's tail engraved all around, rising with revelation-fire from the cedar wood. Fall-down taps the boy's shoulder with the snake's tongue.

"Youth-man, no school last week?"

The boy pushes the roach brigade with his shoe.

"I never have no bus money," he says.

"Where your mother?"

"She home with the new baby," the boy says, the roach on its back, "But go cross-question someone else. Leave me alone."

Fall-down looks away and taps his cane on the sidewalk three times. The traffic light turns green and wind plays at a woman's dress as she crosses the street. A group of schoolchildren crowd into a bus.

"Is me deliver the baby," the boy says after the light turns red then green again, "A little girl with a purple mouth."

"And your mother?"

At the mention of his mother, the boy looks away, suddenly disturbed.

"She alright?"

A blind woman with a cane walks by. She taps around the boy's feet, then continues into the crowd.

"Is what happen?"

"I leave her sleeping," say the boy.

"Angel come?"

Down the road, the blind woman taps her steps over cracks in concrete, wondering at the mixed scent of death and afterbirth on the boy's clothes.

"Why is only fallen angel full up Jamaica?" the boy says. "What happen to all the rest of the angel-them—Cupid and ting? And archangel!" There are tears in his eyes.

"Never mind, youth-man," Fall-down says, and he takes the shoe brush out of the satchel he carries and reaches for the boy's feet.

"Watch me shine your shoes till you see your true face in them."

The boy kicks his foot and moves away.

"No!"

But Fall-down grabs a hold of him and holds his feet to the ground with strong hands. The boy begins to cry; there is a pain inside like the bass hunger in his make-believe guitar. A newspaper vendor nearby calls out to Fall-down, "Leave him! Leave the boy!" But then, seeing the shoe brush on the ground, resumes counting her coins. Helpless, the boy lets go, leans into the zinc; and Fall-down begins to clean—ceremoniously—because angels, even fallen ones, do everything with devotion and complete munificence.

The little brass Africas clink-clink as Fall-down breaks a twig from the tamarind tree behind the fence, scrapes mud from the crevices of the rubber soles. An old rag dipped into a water bottle comes next. Fall-down proceeds careful as wiping an infant's bottom. He pulls a tin of black shoe polish from his pocket, sniffs the varnish for quality before spreading it with small even strokes. And then comes the brush—the bristles from an old stallion.

"Tell me when you can see your face," he says.

He works the brush until little beads of sweat form on his forehead. The boy's feet are broad and flat and he has worn down both his heels; there is a tiny hole on the left toe and the laces are frayed. None of this stops Fall-down; he polishes and buffs as if life itself depends on the shoes' shine.

"You can see your face yet?"

The boy opens his eyes and looks at his shoes.

"No, Ras," he says.

The boy is thinking about the purple-lip baby his mother pushed into his hands. How he left them both on the bed and ran for help down the road. There had been a tune playing on the radio, something about Zion and needing to get there. By the time he came back with the neighbour-woman, his mother had already stopped breathing. Her white nightgown was wrapped around her like egg skin, the crying baby still between her legs, its purple-flower lips all quiver-quiver; and the radio going /dub revo/lution/music to rock the na/tion. All night the boy chopped a path to Fall-down's Zion, willing his mother to find her way to that guava-ripe place. The Riva-mumma with the blue-skin skirt would meet her there. She would show his mother her new Zionself in the clear river-bottom water.

"You can see your face yet?"

The boy looks down at his shoes and sees the reflection of Fall-down's little brass Africas shimmering back and forth.

"You see your face?"

"Yes, I see mi face," he says.

Evening comes and the Kingston sky is pink and orange behind the billboards and electric poles. Fall-down pokes the boy's back with the end of his staff. He has fallen asleep on the overturned bucket, dreaming of a shell in the Queen of Sheba's navel. He is just about to steal it, when Fall-down wakes him. He rubs his eyes. Never mind, in his next dream, he will find his mother in the hospital freezer and put the Queen's cowrie in her cold navel.

Out on the road there is an accident—a truck moving at full speed catches on sagging cable wires, pulling down electric poles with a panic of breaks and backed-up traffic.

"Oh Absalom, Absalom!" Fall-down shouts.

"Who?"

The boy still rubs his eyes. His mind is on his mother and he has no time for madman talk. The hospital put her in the morgue; there was no money for a funeral. Eventually her unclaimed body will be sent to the university where the young doctors will cut her up for their studies. Someone will drill along the sutures of her skull, separate the small bones of her ear, slice her liver with a silver blade, dissect her heart—unaware of the secret place in an upper chamber where she has written the boy's name.

"But look all this time and I don't even know how them call you," Fall-down says. "What you name, youth?"

"Delroy."

"Who you name after?"

The boy shrugs his shoulders.

"One day you will get a new name," Fall-down says.

"And you, Ras?"

"Negus. My true name is Negus."

RASTAMAN, 1978

Something Bout Leenah
[Electric Guitar]

"Bob Marley isn't my name. I don't even know my name yet."
June, 1974

Well ... me like Leenah. Me like the dawta. Me like how her hands make reggae. That dawta can reason bout a drop of water or an ant or a stone. When me look on her, her eyes make four with mine; a she-lion. Me like that. Check this. One night in London, I&I dream she know mi true name. No joke. She was wearing a red dress and she smell like blood. Woman-blood. She come to me and she whisper mi name in mi ears. It write down in a book, she say. And she tell me the page and the name of the book. When I&I wake up, I forget what she tell me. But from that, me crazy for her. Me want her. Me thirst for her like how fire thirst for blood. But something bout Leenah. The groove right, but the time never right. The place never right. But me enjoy her still, you know? When London grey, you need a dawta like that.

England is a morgue, Rasta. Listen, after one year a London, me tired a that scene. England come in like America. I live a Delaware one time. America, the mouth of the dragon to rhaatid. I work few months as a welder. Me couldn't live inna that place. Tribulation, Rasta. I go on tour, but me couldn't live inna it. You understand. Everywhere you turn, you buck gainst Babylon. Law for this, law for that, where to piss, where not to piss. I-man don't deal with law. I-man is Rasta. I-man lawless. Check this. Is America this: mow you lawn, pull out the weeds, stay in line, don't get outta line, park your car here, don't park it there, don't holler in the street, don't do this, don't do that. One time Babylon stop I and cross-question I, say I cross street on red light. Bull shit. I-man is a African. I-man cross for the trinity—red green and gold. No man own I&I feet. I walk when I ready. Wake up people! Stand up for your rights. Is long time Rastaman a warn you and you nah listen. Wake up, Zion. Wake up! When them tell you to go right, you go left; when them tell you sing high, you sing low.

And look how things funny. We can't stop run. We can't stop. We run from one Babylon, find the next one. Breddren and sistren, hear me now—until we find-back Africa, until we find Zion, we can't leave captivity. Dig? Rastafari.

Prince Asfa Wossen, His Majesty son, him contact me while me was in London. Look a man like that, the son of the Most High, have to run from him owna country because Babylon inna the very court of the Elect of Jah. Them woulda kill him! Tell me, Rasta, what sense it make.

Well, me no know why the prince give me him faadah ring, but him see something inside-a me, and him give me it. Seen? When him give me the ring, me never put it on right away. Me too shock. Is after him leave, me put it on and feel it heavy on mi finger. Is the ring the Most High used to wear on him left hand. Causa that now, me wear it on my right. For how I could presumptuous as to wear it on the left? Me fraid a this ring, Rasta. This ring no I-levate I, it humble I. From that time on, I&I realize say my life not in my own hands. Is in the hands of the Almighty, Rasta. People! Don't look to me. Me is the messenger, but a no me the message. The message is Zion. A the message that.

Now that woman, Leenah, she know. I like how she stand up to me. Check her out. She look me in me eye and she listen me with her heart. Me respect her. Me find meself a tell her things me never tell no other woman. Or man. Jah descend on that dawta and she see me plain—no locs and no guitar; no herb and no mic—just I&I.

LEENAH

Kingston, 1978: Exodus

I returned to Jamaica the same year as Bob. My Auntie died and left me £400 and old Austin Cambridge; I sold the car and bought a ticket for home. I enrolled in UWI; rented a room from an elderly woman, Miss Ivy, in Mona. I kept her yard raked, and fed her cat; the rent was cheap. The 1976 shooting incident at Hope Road that had driven Bob away from Jamaica had blown over—well, sort of. When he visited one evening, Miss Ivy eyed him carefully from the enclosed veranda. He knocked on the front gate with a stone and she called, "Is who?" stepping closer to better look. A little dog began to bark, knocking down a bunch of oleanders in a pot.

"Have no fear," Bob said, "it is I."

Miss Ivy relaxed when she saw the twinkle in his eye, opened the padlock and let him in.

"Evening, Madda," he said.

She was an old woman but knew all about Bob, his music, his ganja and the gunshots at 56 Hope in '76.

"I don't want no trouble today, you hear?" And she showed him to my room.

Bob visited only twice, and both times on the run to somewhere else. Jah-Jah work was calling and, anyway, he was used to pretty women coming to him, not the other way around. Still, there was something which made him unable to let me go.

"Mind education don't turn you into a damn fool," he said, rifling through my books.

"Not with you keeping me in check," I said.

I noticed that he was wearing a bandage on one foot, that he walked with a slight limp.

53

"What they do to you now?"

"The raasclaat toe," he said.

I remembered. He had injured the toe in France during a foot-ball game. But now, as then, he brushed it off. "Rasta live!"—the limp becoming the up-beat in his dread walk. That night I would never have believed the sore had become melanoma.

I poured him a drink and lit up his spliff.

"No problem," I said, "Miss Ivy gone to bed already."

Dawta of Zion-O. He still remembered the song.

It was breezy, the curtains blowing. Miss Ivy's cat watched from the dresser in the corner, while next door in the already-dark, a woman's chemise fell from the clothesline, the yard wet from afternoon rain.

Dawta of Zion, Jah-Jah Zion calling come. The hum in Bob's throat came from afar, from deep underground; I&I felt its vibration beneath my bare feet. We passed the spliff back and forth quietly, the cat purring, smoke rising into the pepper plant on the windowsill.

"I had a dream that I found my mother's loc," I said. "It was buried in my navel and I&I pulled and pull until it all came out."

Bob reached for my hair, brushed two fingers along the length of a long loc.

"I miss my mother is all. Sometimes I feel her—like she rolling my hair in her palm. You believe in duppy?"

"Me believe in evahliving."

"Same thing. Country man like you must know duppy."

"Let me see your navel," he said.

"What for?"

"I want to see it; blow likkle herb on it."

The curtains swayed and Bob leaned over and puffed into my hair. The smoke filled my locs; quickened them. Surrounded by haze, I had the sensation of catching fire. His hand was between my thighs, the metal of his ring against my skin.

Outside a horn honked and the cat jumped off the dresser.

"Rhaatid."

"What?"

It was Peaches. She had followed Bob. The curtains blew white flags through the window.

That was the night, after Bob left, when the angel climbed into my dream, holding his primordial book. By the time he arrived, I had already turned out the lights and pulled the nylon curtains. At first I thought it was Bob come back, but then I saw the silhouette of wings. In the morning I wanted to attribute it all to the lambsbread spliff, but there was the yellow pollen on the sheets to account for, and the scent of pomegranate on my bedclothes. Every night the angel came—for a week. On the last night, I lifted his book, heavy in my hands, and was sure I *heard* the clink-clink of his Africas, and his voice—an abeng—as he paused at the window.

"What is your name?" I asked in the dark.

"Negus," he said. "My name is Negus."

FROM BLOODFIAH, RECORD OF DREAMSLOST

Track 12.0: The High Wind of 1979; or, the Falling of Fall-down

The woman closed the book in her dream and handed it to the angel through the parted curtain. He kissed her hand, then shot away in a rush of dust and light—straight to Mt. Zion High—the book, all woman scent, tucked under his arm. He expected to arrive with quietness, to sit and sniff the pages and record her name with hibiscus ink, but immediately upon landing, his wings exploded like feathers from a king's bed and he felt himself falling.

He fell down through the tail-ends of sour dreams, a shower of white flies, the debris of insurrection and pestilence, the stink of death and, finally, through galloping rain. As the ends of his red scarf parachuted above him, he held onto the book clutching it to his chest. There was a hurricane simmering out at sea and it snatched him by the ends of his sleeves, swirled him into its path. In a torrent of green and blue hummingbird plumes the storm gathered speed as he spun towards its centre, legs and arms flailing, through the open eye.

In the middle of anarchy, it was warm and still. Afloat on his back, the falling-down twirled light as ganja pollen and he wished he could rest never-ending in that balmy place. A refrain of languid fern and the imperviousness of lizards played in his head. He opened his mouth and it filled with mist.

The falling-down had almost forgotten himself when, toward morning, the storm lost power and spat him out, and he fell head first into an impatient sea that frothed and tussled and washed him up onto Hellshire Beach. All day he slept in the hot sun, his ledger book of happen-tings under his head, the red cloth over his body.

HERE-SO; HALF WAY TREE

Mosquito

Now Fall-down stands in the middle of the road directing traffic; his staff points left then right, his earrings bright in the sun.

"No worry, all directions lead to hell!" he calls.

Delroy watches from the sidewalk, looking out at the traffic; the street is busy with shoppers and schoolchildren and workers going about their business, and it occurs to him that he alone has nowhere to go. His auntie and cousins in the country already live ten in one room and do not need another mouth to feed. He watched from a hole in the zinc fence as Auntie took his new sister and left her on the steps of Mt. Ephraim. He crouched there watching babysister all night until Mr. Bishop came and found her. Mr. Bishop so old he hardly heard the baby cry the cry of a lost pea dove, but when he felt a little arm flay against his ankle, he jumped back—"But see here!"—picked her up and held her to the sky. Delroy walked back to town all the way from St. Catherine, his mother in the freezer waiting for someone's silver scalpel. And now, if she doesn't get bury, the student doctors at the hospital will study her, put her liver in a jar. He-only left, he stands at the curb, his empty stomach like a knotted scandal bag inside him.

"Which hell you looking?" Fall-down calls to a woman in a big Volvo. The woman throws away her cigarette and closes the tinted windows.

"You think you in heaven, but you living in hell," Fall-down sings.

He stands in the Volvo's path and stretches his staff a few feet above the ground, inviting the woman to proceed with her car beneath the limbo of his snake. The woman honks her horn as the taxi driver behind begins to honk his; soon Half Way Tree is a cacophony of horns. Fall-down raises his staff like a conductor's baton, throws back his head, laughs, then takes a bow.

"Half-way trick," the boy says as Fall-down steps back on the curb.

But the performance over, Fall-down is suddenly serious again, in that way he has of moving from jester to mystic all in one breath.

"Someone just call me," he says.

"Bout what? All the pretty-pretty mosquitoes in Zion?" the boy mocks, still hoping to sustain a lightness of mood.

Fall-down laughs a bent little laugh then walks away. When he comes back, he is leaning on his staff.

"Listen, I have three thousand years experience that you don't have," he says, and the boy, all quiet, sees that in the space of a moment, time has descended on the fallen one, his eyes drawn wild and god-red.

"Too much ras-man talk," the boy says. "Talk plain," and he takes two steps back, away from the eyes catching fire.

Fall-down looks up at the sky, the horizon lined with billboards and electric poles. As he crosses the street, he hears a voice in his ear: "Rhaatid!" It is full of vexation, a slight huskiness around the edges. He is sure it is Bob's.

"But look how Bob call me, all the way from the other side," he says, his eyes far-off. "He don't find Zion yet?"

"Zion?" says the boy, his words high and lifted up.

"I-thiopia, youth! I-frica!" A dread calls from a mini-bus.

Fall-down cocks his head to the side, listening again for Bob.

"Is true? Zion inna Africa, Ras? Why you never tell me?"

But Fall-down cannot hear. He has already taken off, the brass Africas clinking, past the man selling panties and brassieres, past the street evangelist on the corner.

"And next time, don't tell me bout no foot-slip riva-mumma cave-shit to raas," the boy calls, "or is gun-fire!"

"Rhaatid!" Fall-down hears again in his ear, and this time the angel keeps on walking, and does not come back.

CURFEW

LEENAH

Rasta Angel

The angelman who climbed through the window is my babyfather. But how can I tell this? How can you tell people you slept with a man who climbed through your window? Slut. That slut, Leenah. And how do you say you might have been dreaming when it happened?

My daughter looks like her great grandmother, Miss-Winnie. Every day I check her for signs of wings. Lately, her shoulder blades protrude at an awkward angle. I take her to the doctor and he says it is a rare deformity; in fact, this is his first time seeing such a thing. Not to worry—she is perfectly sound, he says. When she begins to walk and then run, the blades shift inwards and outwards, catching bass rhythm. I watch her run by the sea, and imagine her ascending in flight. I name her Anjahla, my angel. "You are my Rasta angel," I say.

And the doctor is right—she is perfectly sound, and smart too.

"What happen to my father?" she asks me.

"I hardly even knew him."

"You slept with a man you hardly knew?"

In school she is a bright girl who asks the teachers questions they don't know how to answer. Anjahla wants to know how much salt can be held in a teardrop and the weight of a heavy heart. She wants to know the meaning of the star in the middle of a star apple, and why if Jah love is free, people don't want it.

"Where you go and get this child?" Ms. Shawn asks.

Sometimes I see her watching the sky or studying leaves, like she looking for signs. But then again, why not? We live a life of signs and symbols—she already knows Deafooman. To speak

Deafooman, you use your hands, your eyes; every part of your structure. Sometimes, I wonder: What does Anjahla sound like?

"What you sound like?" I ask her.

"I sound like a butterfly catching a breeze," she says.

I like the way she signs "breeze," like someone who understands the true blessing of finding just the right current that will permit lift-off. More than anything, I want to hear my daughter's voice.

"Sing me a song," I say.

And I put my hand-middle against her chest, the way I used to with Bob. I close my eyes and feel her breath go in and out, her I-bration against my palm. I feel her sway, chasing after her breeze.

"Long time ago, your Grandma Vaughn gave me one of her locs," I say. "It was brown and long as love and I put it in an empty milk tin and slept with it under the bed. Every night I talked to it in the dark."

"Were you deaf then, Mama?"

"No, I could hear."

"What did your voice sound like when you were a girl?"

"Like Grandma Vaughn's voice, only little bit softer, and like Gran-Winnie's, only higher."

Anjahla is picking off lint from the bedspread, thinking.

"That loc was a company to me, almost like it could breathe," I say.

"But hair is dead, Mama."

"How can it be dead when it holds your whole story?"

Anjahla lifts one of my locs and puts it gainst her cheek. I open the dresser drawer, take a pair of scissors, cut off the loc and give it to her. My one-daughter coils it, a love-root in her small hands. She holds it like a bang-belly baby, watches it unfurl a little, then rest all quiet. When she looks up at me, her eyes full with water.

"What it would be like to hear my voice, Mama?"

"Like Zion."

"Zion is in Africa; you never even been there."

Her eyes are bright and waiting for my reply.

"There is a Zion, deep inside, that don't need ship or plane," I say.

This is the story I want Anjahla to know. They say my mother, Vaughn, pushed me out into the I-niverse on a night when the moon was yellow. My eyes were the same moon colour—jaundice, the midwife said. I had long fingers, like Anjahla, and ears with no lobes; I was named after my great-grandmother, Murlina, who was born in Guinea and came to Jamaica via Cuba on a fishing boat. Murlina was the name given to her by a Spanish captain.

In Cuba, Great-grandmother Murlina had six children, none of them living passed two months. When her seventh, Hector—my grandfather—was born, the Santería priestess said, "Sail south," and that was how Murlina and her husband, Augusto, crossed sea in a fisherman's small boat—Hector curled in an uncle's felt fedora—a parting gift for the ninety-mile journey.

They arrived in Jamaica late-evening, at a place where a quiet river met the sea. A woman washing in the brackish water came to greet them. People say they spoke little English and my great-grandmother, pointing to herself and to her husband and to their crying child and to the open sea, said, "I and I." Many years later, hearing this story I would joke that my great-grandmother, Guinea-woman, Murlina, was the first Rasta. It was 1892, the same year that Haile Selassie—Tafari Makonnen—was born in Ejersa Goro, Ethiopia.

FROM THE HUMMING OF LIONS IN THE GARDEN OF JAH

[Tafari in Bass]
Track 7.0: 1892: Yeshimebet and Her Only Son [Version]

They say Tafari was a soft-spoken child. Even as a baby, though his cry was small, he had an uncanny ability to mesmerize humans and animals alike. Once his mother, Yeshimebet, left him in his cradle, and when she returned, he was holding communion with a magpie; the magpie had a worm in its beak and was feeding it to the boy-child's open mouth. Only when Yeshimebet ran to him did Tafari begin to cry, his arms reaching for the bird flying out into the garden.

Yeshimebet knew that her son was a long-awaited child. She could trace his roots through a line of kings all the way to Makeda and Solomon, the tribe of Judah, the root of Jesse. And now if his father, Ras Makonnen, could raise him so, his son would one day be the 225th emperor of Ethiopia. Yeshimebet had watched as sugar ants made a circle around Tafari's bed, and had seen them march away when Tafari pointed to the open door; she had watched as swallowtails kept vigil at his window, and heard hyenas purr like kittens on the night of his birth. But even then, she had no way of knowing that one day, in a little salt and sugar island fraught with sufferation, her son would be known as God-self Almighty Jah.

FROM BLOODFIAH, RECORD OF DREAMSLOST

Track 3.0: Harar, Ethiopia, 1901: Tafari, the Dreamer

Tafari, the young Judah-lion, had a dream once that a man gave him a song. He was nine years old at the time and had fallen asleep in the eucalyptus garden, his lesson book on his belly. In this dream, he walked down a dirt path thick with fern and red hibiscus. Emerald lizards watched from amid croton leaves, and sea lapped in a quiet cove in the distance. Just as Tafari thought he had stumbled upon paradise, he saw a great throng of wailing children coming toward him. The children were barefoot and dirty, their feet caked with mud; they had left their families and crossed hill and gully to meet the Ethiopian youth in his dream. Upon each child's forehead was written the name, *Ras Tafari*, in black coal. Tafari was just a boy and had not yet been given the title, ras, so he held up his hands as if to say, No, but the children pressed closer and wailed even louder, while from their midst rose the figure of a man with hair like a lion's mane, and a guitar slung over his shoulder. The man sang a strange music that filled Tafari's body with god-fire and sent him dancing through the throng, the children calling, Ras Tafari!

And such as dreams are, many years later the boy-turned-Conquering-Lion, Haile Selassie-I, visited Jamaica at the invitation of the prime minister, and only then, at the doorway of the jet, twirling a ring on his finger and looking out at the greeting throng chanting his name, did he remember the dream and the feel of god-fire.

FROM THE ANGEL'S LEDGER BOOK

[Wood Bongo Cross-rhythms]

ONE LOVE PEACE CONCERT; JAMAICA NATIONAL STADIUM, KINGSTON/APRIL 22, 1978

When Bob Marley sings his voice is guango dread, cacao memory and lions roaring in His Majesty's garden.

The people are hungry for food, for shelter, for Zion; for a leader to part the Red Sea and lead the boat ashore.

The Jamaica National Stadium is electric. Lizards feel the vibration of sound as far as Spanish Town. Even a boy being hanged from a tree in 1766 feels it.

Prime Minister Manley and opposition leader, Seaga, join hands. Bob Marley makes them. There is scent of Leenah on his sleeve.

I want to tell humans: there is more than what the eye sees.

This night, there is a gate to Zion in the Jamaica National Arena. No one finds it, but later a young boy, alone in a Kingston gully, remembers a certain chord in Bob's voice, and sings it into a long-long thread that takes him to a place which is both far and near as his own breath.

LEENAH

The One-foot Woman

The story goes that my grandfather, Hector, married Winnie, an obeahman's daughter. Grandpa Hector was a tailor, a quiet man who liked to smoke a little herb now and then down by the river. That's what Gran-Win told me. She said nobody knew about Hector's herb except she. He liked to smoke while he sewed, his tape measure around his neck. He took an interest in Marcus Garvey, Jah prophet, who went to America preaching back-to-Africa and stirring up so much dust that Babylon had to devise a way to kick him out and deport him to Jamaica—mail fraud, they claimed. Hector wallpapered the two rooms in which they lived with newspaper clippings and drawings of the Black Star Line, Garvey's ships, which would take us to Ghana. That's what I remember most about Gran-Win's house—the ships, and the walls covered with newspaper; it was the same house I grew up in. Gran-Win made a paste of flour and water to stick everything up; I loved her pitchy-patchy.

"I knew Marcus when he was just a boy in short pants," Gran-Win used to say. "Even then, he rub his chin when he talk."

She pasted a note to one wall along with two old calendars that advertised Murray's Miracle Hair Pomade and Palmolive soap. The note went like this: *A little Epsom salt in riverwata and a stone at the battom of the cup two night raw moon and a good night sleep on a bare mattrass see if you find …* After that the ink was too faint to read. I loved Gran-Win's shaky join-up writing, and always wondered what the thing was that needed to be found.

Gran-Win said Grandpa Hector was the one who added a world map, some UNIA pamphlets and bits and pieces of news that had been saved in a Cuban cigar box under the bed. He drew a blue line on the map—Jamaica to Africa—and stuck a threaded needle in his destination. Gran-Win said that first thing every morning he boiled a cup of mint and drank it while studying the wall. He used a piece of magnifying glass, studying each and every one of Garvey's words, admiring the look of Africa in print. LOOK TO AFRICA, the wall said, FOR THE CROWNING OF A BLACK KING. HE SHALL BE THE REDEEMER.

One day Anjahla will tell this story to her children.

It's true Hector carried pictures of Garvey's Black Star Line in his front pocket, but his most valued possession was his Singer sewing machine. Sometimes Winnie thought he loved the sewing machine more than her, more than his own flesh and blood. He had bought it on trust, putting five shillings in a brown envelope every month-end and paying at the post office. He was a good tailor and always had work, sewing way into the night. The sewing machine was his mistress and rum bottle. Whenever something bothered him, he turned to his machine. "Millicent," he called her. When he stitched with Millicent he took off his shoes and socks, because he liked his bare feet against the cool iron of her peddle. It was to Millicent Hector turned when he discovered that the Black Star Line was going nowhere and that Garvey, his vision unsupported, had left for England. Gran-Win said that when Hector sang with Millie that night, his voice was wood-smoke and Job's tears.

HECTOR

Singerman in Root Bass

One thousand stitch will hem a jacket, three hundred a sleeve; not that I count them, but I know them are there. A man don't count his breath, but he know is there. I listen the stitches that way. One stitch at a time, like the words-them on the wall, one word at a time. How many words in this house? Too many to count; this house made of words. And while I stitch I breathe and while I breathe I sing.

Breddren and sistren, I pass through some things in life. When me was a boy, my eyes at my knee, my mother put me on a bus and send me to Spanish Town to spend time with my uncle and learn to sew. When I get off the bus it was night and nobody to meet me. I wander three days and three nights before I find my uncle yard. When I reach the house, I find him dead at his sewing machine, black fly already at his mouth-corner. But the thing about his mouth that I always member was the smile. He dead with a smile on his face. True that. I'm a man don't fraid death, for the first dead I see had a smile on him face.

Now, because my uncle dead, is me teach meself how to sew. One stitch at a time. That's how I learn it. Anything you want learn, you can learn it one thing at a time. One-one cocoa fill basket. I love to sew because it mellow me. And the herb too. It mellow me. If it wasn't for the sewing and the herb, I would be a different man— because I go through some things, I tell you.

My wife, Winnie, the obeahman daughter, she can tell you. Her father set duppy on me because him never want me marry her. But me know Winnie was to be my wife from me was fourteen years old. Me see her a catch water by the river and me see how she set

69

the pan on her head and hold her neck high, her neck so long and straight and pretty make you want kiss it. I used to walk behind her, just so I could watch that neck—and her bottom when she walk. I never realize her father—Bro. Mo—see me watch her from his corner-eye till, one night, him send the duppy of one of them old-time overseer to whip me. The overseer duppy whip me and whip me just like times of slavery. And when him whip me, him say, Who do you love? His voice big and boom. And I say, Winnie. And him say, Who do you love? And I say, Winnie. And still him don't stop till one night something come to me and I say, Long live the Queen, Sar. And then him let me go.

In the morning, not a sign on my back. I get to find out that the overseer was a man used to name Brighton. He was an Englishman on a plantation in Clarendon—but what in them times they used to call Vere. After his wife dead of dengue fever, he go mad and turn blame on Jamaica, and he whip every last slave, every Jack man, woman and child out their bed—5 people dead that night—then he hang himself on a stinking toe tree. Some night when Brighton whip me, my mother stand in the doorway, watching me bawl, but she couldn't do a thing. And when I can't take it anymore I say, Long live the Queen, Sar, and sometime him stop and sometime that don't satisfy neither. On those nights, I have to salute to every duke and duchess and lord and lady, and puss and dog go straight back. You never see Brighton, you know, you only hear the whip and his voice rolling like a three-wheel mill. But my mother knew it was Bro. Mo set Brighton on me, but she couldn't do a thing.

No matter where I go, Brighton follow me. Even after Bro. Mo dead and I marry Winnie and in bed with my wife as a man ought be, Brighton still cast his whip on my back same way. Sometimes I so shame, I don't want Winnie know say Brighton down on me with his whip, and when I cry out I make her think is she and her sweet why I holler. For we fight not against flesh and blood, but principalities and powers. Is there a balm in Gilead?

Then the thought came to me that if I could go Africa, Brighton could never follow me there, and that's when I hear about Marcus Mosiah Garvey and his ships to Zion.

RASTAMAN

[Acoustic Guitar]

2:19 AM; May 15, 1978; quiet quarter-moon; back door—56 Hope
Rd., Kingston 6

> Zion train
> Zion train
> Zion train
> Oh Children—

LEENAH

But Garvey's Black Star Line went broke and the ship, old and leaky-leaky, never made it to Africa at all. Second chance came on a sticky afternoon when Gran-Winnie met a man at a standpipe by the road as she waited for slow water to fill her cup. He said his name was Leonard Howell. He had quick, intelligent eyes, and a beard alive with natty hair; he gave her a postcard of His Imperial Majesty, Haile Selassie I, Emperor of Ethiopia. "Wake up and live," Mr. Howell said; then he was gone. The emperor in the photo was handsome with his crown and velvet robe; Winnie had never seen a black king before. With his arch eyebrows and long nose, he looked like Uncle Lloyd on her mother's side. She ran home to Hector—"Come see a man!" She had found the king prophesied in the writing on the wall.

Rumour had it that the emperor's photo was good for passage on a ship back to Africa. Hector arrived at Kings Street Wharf on October 14, 1934 with the postcard from Howell, a suitcase containing a change of clothes, five pounds in his pocket and the brown fedora he had crossed sea in as a newborn. He was going to Africa. He would send for Winnie and the children once he got settled. The dock was scattered with men just like himself; most of them beardsmen—they called themselves Rastas. They had all felt Ethiopia in their marrow, paid their shilling and answered the call. But passage to Africa was nowhere to be found and when the authorities came, it was clear that no one would be leaving for Ethiopia that day. Bit by bit the men dispersed. Hector alone sat on the dock until the next morning, when he took the bus home, his fedora in his suitcase. As Winnie made him chicken-foot soup that afternoon, the house was quiet. She set the table with bowls that had belonged to Guinea-woman, Murlina.

"Your passage soon come," she said.

After that, Hector took in more and more sewing and began to pedal his way to a far off place only he could see. Sometimes when he sewed on his beautiful black machine, he was taken so far away that when Gran-Win called, he could barely hear her. He sewed through hurricane, through hogs in labour under the house, through visitations of dark moths, and Gran-Win's praying; his beard gone natty dread-o. They say my mother, Vaughn, was born at a neighbour's house across the hill on a night when the moon had been eaten up and Hector stayed home to sew. Later, on his way to see his new daughter, he heard the news that Garvey had moved to London, his Zion dream unsupported.

It was when Garvey died, and on a day that Hector had come back from his usual trip to the post office, that he disappeared—both he and the sewing machine. He had been such a quiet man, no one understood why he would leave. One day, many years later, Gran-Winnie would tell me that Hector ran off with a one-foot woman, Millicent, black as the Ace of Spades.

Revelation of Wisdom According to Jah Prophets (1:20)

(For Leenah had no way of knowing that on the day he made his last payment at the post office, her grandfather, Hector, journeyed all the way to Zion on his foot-pedalled sewing machine. His tape measure around his neck, he pedalled and the machine whirred; pedalled and whirred into the night. For it is possible to arrive at Zion, one stitch at a time, especially if the thread is cerulean-blue and you are stitching your finest suit. On such a needle-and-thread journey, you forget the children still playing outside, the cup of cerasee cooling on the kitchen table, the newspaper headline, "Black Star Liner." What need is there for a ship to cross sea when your Singer hums across an expanse of blue, your feet pedalling over the shoes of saints and charlatans and galaxies of the fallen, to the marvellous equations of the long-dead and the divination of spilt rice? When you finish the last seam, the far future arrives, like the piece of thread caught in your mouth, the little house in which you sit, lit up by a home-sweet-home lamp on the sill, two men outside your window—one a prophet, the other a Judah-lion—the nutmeg tree shaking in anticipation.)

STUDIO Z: MT. ZION
HECTOR

TRACK 2.5: Singerman Nyahbinghi Chorus

How many stitches to balm I back? One stitch at a time.
How many stitches to holy Mt. Zion? One-one at a time.
If you can't go by ship, you go by spirit; if you can't go by ship,
you go by spirit. You stitch and you stitch till you run out
of thread, but you stitching same way. Yes, you stitching same
way. And that's when you know that you reach Zion Gate.
The feet of the defiled cannot enter therein. Cannot
enter therein—

FROM THE ANGEL'S LEDGER BOOK

[Wind Fall at 33½ Rotations per Minute]

Sound Day, 2001—"I am not mad: I am introducing God." Lee Scratch Perry, the Upsetter, *speaks these words.*

Madness is rampant on this island. The mad dream dreams and have visions. They stand on street corners and tell it. No one listens.

The mad are the best lovers. The angel knows this.

The sane are the worst lovers (unless they are sane in an asymmetrical way).

Sanity can be both asymmetrical and symmetrical. Likewise, madness can also be both asymmetrical and symmetrical. Two related sides of different tunes.

Jesus Christ was 33 years old when he rose from the dead. The temporal lobe in his right hemisphere picked up a reverb, ricocheted down fire—Krishna, Buddha, Allah, Jah-Jah; Krishna, Buddha, Allah, Jah-Jah; Krishna, Buddha, Allah, Jah-Jah—and he remembered why he had come.

33 is a symmetrical number which tends to bring asymmetrical outcomes of both the sane and mad. 33½ is its tipping point.

Summer Solstice, 1887—The sewing needle on Emil Berliner's phonograph reads the grooves on a metal disc.

March 21, 1940—A man in a little district in Jamaica hums as he sews 33½ stitches per minute with blue thread.

DUB-SIDE CHANTING

Track 11.0: Ampersand

The smoke clears, and H.I.M. sits on a stone in the yard and eats sugarcane. Bob looks around at the little hill. It is covered with crab grass; a mosquito lands on his forehead.

"This place, this Dub-side; is where I&I reach?"

H.I.M. smiles with no teeth, but says nothing. For there are places of the soul not even the Rastaman knows. Places only I-magination can see. The little ampersand of Bob's I&I fastens and unfastens its latch. Bob opens his mouth and the words rush—&I–I&I–I&I&—

From a far-far away place, there is an echo of an echo of the whir of a sewing machine—

"That's Hector," says H.I.M. "He arrived at Studio Z. pedalling, and has not stopped sinth. He thinks if he stops he will fall down the mountain to 1940 where he began."

"Is true he will fall?"

H.I.M. shrugs.

"For him, sewing and Zion are the same thing. And who am I to say otherwise? There is a Zion which is a place deep inside."

Bob listens with wistfulness to the faint whir-whir. He climbed Mt. Zion once while strumming guitar. He wished he could have stayed there. He notices the yard. There is a goat tied to a wood fence and a hen pecks at crushed corn. The nutmeg tree is visible now, but beyond it hills extend into miles and miles of more hills, and more nutmeg and bamboo, and there is no trace at all of the whoosh of his arrival. He wonders how in the name of Almighty Jah he could have arrived at the right hand of Haile-I without the ring. Its return to the Almighty's finger was to mark the completion of his work, he is sure. Without it, how else is he to prove that he has been a dutiful son of the Most High? He looks over at H.I.M. enjoying his sugarcane and marvels at his calm.

"Rhaatid."

H.I.M. watches from his rock on the other side of the yard, spits cane trash into an empty tin.

"Do not be discouraged," he says, setting down the tin. "Thuch rings have been lost and found before. And thuch stories have been told before. This is not your purpose."

Bob picks up a stone and hurls it across the hill. "Bloodclaat!"

STUDIO Z

Track 7.5: The Man in the Brown Fedora

And Hector pedals and stitches, an exultant smile on his face, his feet moving without effort.

FROM THE HUMMING OF LIONS IN THE GARDEN OF JAH

Track 5.0: Jah Bless [Version-Version]

They say the angel, Negus, was there when Boaz slept with the Moabitess, Ruth. And Ruth begat Obed and Obed begat Jesse and Jesse begat David. And the angel was there when David watched Bathsheba, the Hittite's wife, bathing on the roof-top. And Bathsheba begat Solomon and Solomon longed for sons. The angel was there when King Solomon made love to the Queen of Sheba. Rasta live.

They say Solomon was smitten with desire, but the Queen had a hoof, and he was afraid of it. With a stroke of courage, he kissed his ring and put it to her lips; and at its touch, a flame ignited in her mouth and moved all the way down through her woman temple. It would be the only time in her life she would swallow fire.

Queen Makeda knew she was pregnant by the persistent itch at her coccyx and the bitter taste in her mouth. Her hoof was gone and, without it, she felt tired and groggy, anxious to return to her native land. Before her departure, King Solomon gave her a ring with his royal seal—a lion raising a brazen tail. She thought, perhaps it could be the one from the night before—but she was not certain; at its touch, the flame had entered her body, filled her with heat and she had no remembrance of its markings, only the scent of jasmine on Solomon's hand.

"Give this ring to the child when it is born," he said.

She left for the nine-month journey home to Abyssinia, across desert and mountain, in wind and rain. The boy-child was called Bayna-Lehkem. He was born with a full set of teeth, eyebrows like two dark caterpillars and his father's high forehead. Queen mother bathed him in a basin of warm water, the golden ring resting at the bottom. Later, she fell asleep as he suckled at her breast and she dreamt of her boy-child grown tall and stalwart and of his children and his children's children, a line of kings and queens two hundred and twenty-five strong, marching with deliberation into the future. She approached the last—an old man in strange clothing, small in stature, a little dog barking at his feet.

"What is your name?" she asked him.

"No one knows what it really is," he replied.

"But what do they call you?"

"The Lion of Judah," he said. "I am the last emperor, Haile Selassie of Ethiopia. I alone am left."

And he held up his right hand, a ring with a brazen-tailed lion on his finger.

Selah.

DUB-SIDE CHANTING

Track 16.0: The Scent of Nutmeg

H.I.M. picks bits of cane trash from his clothing; looks over at Bob.

The nutmeg tree inhales; there is a little shift in the air.

"If you insist, there is one possibility of return," he says.

Bob looks up.

"You can exchange places with a fallen angel." There are faint lines on H.I.M.'s forehead as he looks away at the hills. "But be prepared to accept the consequences."

Away-away in Babylon, there is left-over election blood on the sidewalk; a baby suckles at a dog's teat; the meat in the market is soon rotten.

"You will have seven days, but this time, don't expect to return on the wingth of death. You will need to find Zion's undisclosed gate—your heart will tell you where it is; such gates are different for each of us. Do all this; then return here."

Lulu has fallen asleep on the steps of the little house. Crickets soprano in the hills.

"And if I don't find it?"

"At the end of seven days, you remain in Babylon—a fallen one on the street."

Bob is quiet, contemplating the flicker in the

home-sweet-home lamp; then he rubs his chin and looks His Majesty in the eye.

"I&I am about my father's business."

The air in the yard is pungent with the nutmeg tree's exhale. Somewhere, Hector keeps on pedalling; cerulean-blue thread caught in his mouth.

THE DAY AND THE HOUR ARE DECIDED AND BOTH PROPHET
AND FALL-DOWN STAND AT THEIR DESIGNATED PLACES —
FALL-DOWN INSIDE THE CLOCK TOWER AT HALF WAY TREE
AND BOB ON A ROCK AT THE BOTTOM OF STUDIO D. FALL-
DOWN OPENS THE DOOR TO THE CLOCK TOWER WITH THE
SET OF KEYS HE CARRIES IN HIS CANVAS BAG. HE HAS KEYS
TO THE CLOCK TOWERS IN ALL THE TOWN SQUARES IN
JAMAICA — HALF WAY TREE, MAY PEN, MANDEVILLE, PORT
ANTONIO, OLD HARBOUR — YOU NAME IT, FOR SUCH MIS-
CELLANY IS THE PRIVILEGE OF A FALLEN ANGEL. IT IS RARE
THAT ANY OF THE GRAND CLOCKS WORK. MOST ARE THE
MARK OF THE ENGLISH, AND NO ONE SEEMS TO WANT TO
REMEMBER THE ENGLISH. THEY STAND IN THE SQUARES
LIKE NEGLECTED OLD MEN. FALL-DOWN LOOKS BOTH WAYS,
THEN OPENS THE PADLOCK ON THE CLOCK TOWER AND
STEPS INSIDE, CLOSING THE DOOR BEHIND HIM. THERE IS
A FAINT SMELL OF URINE FROM DOGS AND MEN RELIEVING
THEMSELVES AT THE BASE OF THE TOWER. HE TAKES OFF
HIS CLOTHES AS HE HAS BEEN INSTRUCTED.

*

BOB KNOWS THE ROCK AT THE NEVA-EDGE OF THE DUB-SIDE
WHEN HE FINDS IT — HIS FINGERS TRACE THE LETTERS EN-
GRAVED IN ITS SIDE, JAH RASTAFARI. THIS IS THE PLACE
WHERE H.I.M. LAYS HIS HEAD WHEN HE DREAMS OF LIONS
SINGING REDEMPTION. BOB HAS ARRIVED WITH ONLY A
DENIM SHIRT, A PAIR OF TROUSERS AND RED GREEN GOLD
UNDERPANTS. HE TAKES THE CLOTHES OFF NOW, FOLDS
THEM CAREFULLY AND LAYS THEM ON THE ROCK AT THE
PRECISE MOMENT WHEN DOWN IN BABYLON IN THE CLOCK
TOWER THE FALLEN ANGEL FOLDS HIS. SOMEONE KISSES

BOB ON HIS RIGHT SHOULDER, AND WHEN HE TURNS HE SEES AN OLD WOMAN, SO BEAUTIFUL IN HER AGE — HER DREADLOCS LONG AND WHITE AS MADAM FATE FLOWERS, HER SKIN AS COPPER, HER EYELASHES LIKE THE ANTENNAE OF BUTTERFLIES. WHEN SHE SMILES HER TEETH REVEAL THE WORDS, FOOL'S GATE, WRITTEN IN DARK LETTERS. SHE KISSES HIM AGAIN, THIS TIME ON THE MOUTH.

"GO NOW, GO," SHE SAYS.

IN THE DARK OF THE CLOCK TOWER, FALL-DOWN FEELS THE SAME LIPS AND SMELLS THE SAME SWEETNESS OF COMPELLANCE BEHIND THE WOMAN'S EARS. HE CLOSES HIS EYES, TAKEN BY HER KISS, HIS HAND SUDDENLY IN HER WHITE HAIR, THE OTHER REACHING BENEATH HER STAR FLOWER SHOULDER STRAP. SHE PULLS AWAY FROM HIM, SHAKING A LONG FINGER. "TSK, TSK," THE WORDS, SECOND CHANCE, ACROSS HER TEETH.

FALL-DOWN LOOKS AROUND TO FIND HIMSELF ON A HILL OF CRABGRASS AND HIBISCUS FLOWERS. HERE HE IS — NAKED IN A GARDEN OF DELIGHTS, HIS MEMBER DISTENDED — THE BEAUTIFUL WOMAN DISAPPEARED.

"I NO LUCKY AT ALL," HE SAYS OUT LOUD.

HERE-SO; HALF WAY TREE

In the Clock of Babylon

Down in the clock of Babylon, Bob opens his eyes to darkness. He fumbles around in the closed space and finds Fall-down's clothes folded in a corner. A shoe, big as jackfruit, surprisingly fits his foot perfect. In Fall-down's body he has the feeling that he is standing on Jonkanoo stilts. In the opposite corner there is a canvas bag and a wooden staff; he picks them up and feels around for the door. The latch is rusty and moves only after pushing against it with all his weight. He stumbles outside into Half Way Tree and instantaneously has no memory of the Judah ring or why he has returned to Babylon at all. He has seven days to return to the right hand of Jah, that's all he knows.

The night is starless and balmy; the streets almost empty except for three youths walking home from a party, and a drunk man wailing in front of the post office. A car speeds by and Bob hears his own voice on the stereo, *So Jah sey*; he sings along, the sound from his throat deep and scratchy; there is a clink-clink, at his ears. In the early morning darkness in the middle of the square, he stands and looks to all four directions, then heads up Hope Road on his long legs.

His gate at 56 is locked with a chain. The place is in darkness except for one little light in a room upstairs. He shakes the gate and two dogs come rushing out.

"Rita!" he calls, still surprised at his voice.

"Rita!"

She will recognize him; he is sure. For it was her—even at the hour of his death who had sung background—her soprano wailing pressing him on, straight to the right hand of Jah. "Don't look back!" she had urged, "Don't look back!" And now here he is, back at 56 Hope Road, standing at his own gate, a Fall-down.

"Rita!" he calls.

It is late; the street quiet. A police car slows down in front of the gate.

"Is me—Bob. I looking for Rita, for anybody."

The Babylon laughs and continues on down the road.

*

Back at Half Way Tree there is a young boy alone in the park. He plucks a pretend guitar and make-believe strings vibrate hunger. The frogs in the park hear. Bob hears it too; he walks toward the sound and sits next to the boy.

"I thought you wasn't coming back," the boy says.

A gush of wind and dust from a late truck stirs the brass Africas at Bob's ears.

"Jah send me back," he says.

"What?"

"Seven days inna Babylon, that's all I-man know."

Bob sees that the boy does not understand. He shifts closer and looks into his eyes.

"Is me, Bob. Bob Marley." But his words mean nothing to the youth. "I am about my father's business."

"Don't bother with that," says the boy. He is too tired for joking. Tired of Fall-down and his nonsense. "Where you fly-go and come back now? Zion?"

A bird in the branch above them closes its eyes. The park is still, even the gun-man in the corner asleep.

"The right hand of my faadah," says Bob.

The boy sighs; puts away his guitar.

"Shine mi shoes for me?" He reaches in Bob's satchel and hands him the brush and shoe polish. "I like when you shine mi shoes."

The youth sits with his back against the tree, waiting; and Bob looks at the dented can, the little latch on the side that pops the lid open—the fumes from the polish so strong, it sends a tingle to the top of his head. He used to clean his grandfather, Omeriah's shoes. He shined them nice-nice with a coconut brush and soft cloth, just like Omeriah taught him, for Omeriah said, even the dead should see them face in a shoes that shine right. And this is how Bob has worked all his life—burning midnight oil, tuning voice and word and chord, that even the long-dead higherstand themselves, clear-clear, when they hear his Rastaman chant.

And so it is he shines the boy's shoes with livication; the stiff brush bearing into man-made leather, kneading bone and sinew underneath—this moment everything. The clock on the tower is stuck at five past seven. A lizard stretches its body across the minute hand and the moon waxes to fullness over the park; the fall-down earrings go *Af-rica/Af-rica*.

"You can see your face, youth?"

"Yes, I see mi face," the boy says. And he rests awhile, marvelling at Africa a ting-ting in brass.

Afterwards, the boy pushes his legs in a crocus bag and curls up under the tree.

"I want to sleep with my shoes on," he says. He closes his eyes and pulls the crocus bag higher. "Tomorrow, remember tell me my true name."

Bob watches him sleep. He touches his cheek and wonders at a deep hunger even food cannot fill. There is a hole at the foot of the crocus bag; he covers it with leaves.

Back at the clock, he collapses on the floor and sleeps a sleep in which a girl reads a book. She turns the pages like an ole-time hymnal and with each turning there is a faint nutmeg smell. "What yu reading?" he calls from the other side of the dream. "Is a book of mysteries," she says, without looking up, "be careful—you are in it."

THE MARVELLOUS EQUATIONS OF
THE DREAD

LEENAH

The Season of Expectance

In her sleep Gran-win sometimes heard Hector's feet on the pedal of his sewing machine, *natty dread-oh*. She heard him pause to thread his needle and then start again, always humming a tune of contentment. She kept the space he had occupied with his sewing empty, as if anticipating his return. Even after I was born, she swept and dusted the little corner, refusing to put—for not even a moment—as much as a chair in its place. For a part of her expected that one day Grandpa Hector might return just as mysterious as he had left.

She made sweets, selling to school children—coconut drops, grater cake, gizzada and tamarind balls, and the one Hector had liked the best, busta. Every June 30, the date of Hector's disappearance, she made a plate of sticky busta and put it in his corner. In the morning it would be nibbled down by a sweet-tooth rat or covered with sugar ants, a moth wing stuck to it. And always on that day, my mother, Vaughn, sat on the veranda reading a book, half-waiting for the brown fedora to appear above the red hibiscus and the big smile on her Papa's face as he entered the yard. He would say that he had journeyed to a far-off land and seen signs and wonders, and that now he had come to take her back with him.

The season of expectance ended when Vaughn had a vision.

SISTAH VAUGHN

The Writing on the Wall

For where there is no vision, the sistren perish. Yu see me? I&I is a self-taught woman. I never get much schooling, but I always love to read, and I could sew too. From I small, I never have much, but I learn to read from biscuit paper and sardine tin and from Papa's papers on the wall. LOOK TO AFRICA FOR THE CROWNING OF A BLACK KING —those were the words I learned first; Papa's red pencil-line underneath. When I was a child, no cow jump over the moon for me, no, only Africa and the Black Star Line, the ships to carry us. Years later, I recite that wall like a poem while I nurse Leenah. And give thanks to the Almighty for Mrs. Williams and her mildew and stink magazines full with wood louse. She was the post mistress, you know, but when she hear Miss-Winnie girl love to read, she give me the box and I find a *Negro Chronicle* and a June, 1931 *National Geographic*. I never know it then, but that little book Jah-send, for I turn the cover and find the black king in it, high and lifted up and sitting on his throne, making big news—the crown-nation of His Imperial Majesty, Haile Selassie I, Emperor of Ethiopia in living colour. From the Conquering Lion to the fish of Lake Tsana, I read that thing and take in every word. Soon as I get to the end of the crown-nation, I start again and is like the Africa drums beating and the men with the long bamboo pipes calling, just for I. I&I get to the middle page and I in deep now, for there's a picture of an Ethiopian holding an ostrich egg (and Jah be my judge, she look just like Mama), the egg big like a movie obeah-ball in her hands. I look at that egg and ponder my future. And all the

© Alex Stöcker

HOW WILL YOU HAVE YOUR EGG?

while Mama watching me from her corner eye—Papa and his everlasting sewing-sewing, and now my reading-reading. Is like she just waiting for something to happen: sky to drop, fire to catch, Papa to come. She think I reading, but I mining the egg.

The vision that end the time of expectance came like this:

I was sitting out in the yard, lost in the Ethiopian egg, when a man called, psst, from under the cashew tree. It was Hector, only young-looking and with no crease down the middle of his forehead. Everything hush as he studied me through the eye-&-eye of a silver needle, me like a young lioness he find in a field. When I make to rush to him, he disappear, and stand in his place was a small man in a well-adorn khaki suit and a smile, with a gap between the teeth. He give me a ripe Number Eleven mango from a bowl, and soon as I bite into it and look away, he gone.

Mama listen to me tell the vision and she say right away, That's it, Hector not coming back. She put a croton pot in the space save for his return and wake up that same night with a feeling to sew. Next morning, she go into town and buy three yards of cloth for a new red dress, and cut it and stitch it and sew it by hand and not a woman in Brown's Town hold their head high as she.

That was the same year I turn seventeen and meet Gully. I was so small then, my waist slim like a bamboo. I stand outside a storefront reading the magazine and I see Gully from my cornereye, watching me. After a while he say, "Dawta of Sheba," and I look up and smile—his face dark and his teeth white and line up all pretty; his hair push up in a tam. He had a little picture hang around his neck, and when I look good it was the same-same emperor-man, just how I did vision him. I so frighten to see my vision justa dangle before me, I couldn't stop look. The Most High rise and fall gainst Gully chest and, Jah be my judge, every time the picture rise up is like H.I.M. nodding, Yes, yes. Signs and wonders no come more than that. Three months later, me go live with Gully and me pregnant with Leenah.

"I could see it coming," Mama said. "Mine you get burn."

96

But Gully wasn't like some Rastaman. When him call me his empress, him mean it and him treat me like it too. If Gully have only one orange, him share it with me, and if him reasoning with a breddren, him call me come. "Woman flow like a river and the river is life and life is the source of Jah holiness," he say. Nighttime, he roll my locs and count them and call me Africa. That's how him school I&I, and I&I witness him strength. But listen me good, is not Gully why I turn Rasta. You see me? I didn't follow nobody. I had a vision. *That's* how I turn Rasta.

LEENAH

Years later, Miss-Winnie, my grandmother, would tell me that my parents met in Brown's Town when Vaughn turned the page of an old magazine and contemplated an ostrich egg on a plate. Later, Vaughn tore out the pages and stuck them to the wall. The caption under the ostrich woman: How will you have your egg? So these are the words I sing to Anjahla. I make up a song about a woman with an ostrich egg on a plate. The woman dare not break the egg or else the children will have no vision, and where there is no vision, the people perish. Look-here, I say. The woman holds the egg steady on the plate; she listens for Vaughn, my mother's voice in a far-off wilderness, the nyahmbic beat of a Rastawoman's feet—Sing, Vaughn, sing.

SONG OF VAUGHN

1965 Sistren Speech Piece

I&I is a Rasta woman. I have one hundred and forty-four locs because the square root of a hundred and forty-four is twelve and
twelve is a number perfect as the twelve moons that circle the
twelve gates of the house of Zion. Sometimes when I pile the hundred and forty-four on top my head, the locs-them catch waves
straight outta Zion and is like I carrying Jah-Jah ark on top I&I
head. I&I is a Rasta woman. Is lion-woman I is.

One day I wash my hair and sit down on a rock to let it dry in
the sun and the sun so sweet, I vision a woman with a sceptre of
righteousness in her hand. The woman oil my locs one by one with
an oil sweet as rosemary and each time she oil one, she call me by a
different name. When she finish reason with me, even the very secrets in the belly of the fish at the bottom of the river I coulda see.

But they have some bad-mind people fill up this island. Babylon!
They don't like see a Rasta woman strive. They take me for mad.
They take me for insane, how I wear my dreadfullness and knot
it up nice and trod like an empress on the face of the earth. Bad-
minded people. You have to careful of them.

This is how it all started. They stone my house at night when
me and my babyfather in bed sleeping. Yes! And it wasn't no science stone neither—is bad-minded people do it! Boom-boom, I
hear rockstone coming down on the zinc. Jah! Next day, I rope my
dreads and wrap them up good and hold my head high and step
out like a queen. I wasn't going let those people stop me. Bad-
minded people! Is true they don't want no Rasta in the district.
They think Rasta is backwardness.

But that wasn't the end of it. One day me and Gully go market and them burn down the house, crisp-crisp to the ground. Mighty Jah, what a wickedness. The only thing left was a pair of iron scissors did belong to my father. I take the scissors and I cut off piece of my locs and give it to Leenah and I say, "If anything happen, remember who you is," and I send her to her grannie, not even have a change of clothes to her name. I wasn't going to let them hurt my one-daughter! How you mean?

Me and Gully stay behind with Riva Man. The neighbours mouth-them seal; nobody wasn't telling a thing what them did see. Fear fill them up. Riva Man help us build back the house, and Jah anointing come down on me that even the little pear tree that did scorch, spring back and bear so, till we had was to give some of the fruit away to the very cowards that did stand and watch the house burn.

Now in those days, Riva sell brooms in the market—that's how we meet him. He never really have to help us, but he see how we suffer, and he do it out of the goodness of his heart. That day, when the house finish, I take one of his brooms—just like he show me—and I sweep the twelve corners, each corner twelve times; and the whole time I sweeping, I just calling the twelve names of Jah—the Alpha, the Omega, the Lord of Lords, the King of Kings, the Root of Jesse, the Elect of God, the Conquering Lion of the Tribe of Judah, His Imperial Majesty, Haile-I Selassie-I, The Most High, Jah Rastafari—and the whole time I calling Jah, the bad-minded people-them driving by, watching from their corner eye. One of them even send her puppy-dog to my door with a size twelve science shoes in its mouth! But hear me now—the power of Jah come down in the house and fill me up and cast out the dog. You watch me and them. Rastawoman! I dwell betwixt and between and no evil shall overcome she-lion; yu see me? I hold my neck proud and balance Jah-Jah ark on top I&I head.

LEENAH

1966: Jah Live

"Bring in all Rastas, dead or alive!" That's what the Prime Minister, Bustamante, had said. We were all criminals to them. Too brazen and unmanageable for them. We had found our own God; told our own story; fashioned our I&I language; trod to our own riddim without their consent; held our knotty dreads high; everything on our own terms, I-fiantly.

"Is war then," Papa said. He walked on the street, holding up a sign, *Rasta Live*. People warned him, "Mine you get kill," but he did not care. At night, his bongo drum shook the ground. O–I&I/will ne/va leave dis field/till I vic/tory is won/–O

In the end, because they hated Rasta so, bad-mind Babylon shot Papa down and left him for dead under a tree. Later that night, some drunk youth found him and set him afire. It happened a year after the house burning—I saw the burnt tree stub with my own two eyes. I wondered whether Papa was still alive when he catch fire. There is a history on this island of trees bearing witness. Did Papa die with a word at his tongue like the boy at the silk cotton? If trees could talk.

A boy at school boasted how he saw Papa's head on the ground, black as roast breadfruit, only it didn't smell that way. He said it smelled of roast-dog. I couldn't stand that boy. Afterwards in Kingston, and later London, when the smell of my burnt hair came back to me, it would be mixed with roast-dog. I remember vomiting on the train once, the stink on my coat was so bad.

Even after the burning, Mama held her head high. I have a feeling she did not always feel as strong as she made out to be. But she could fool anyone, the way she balanced that ark on her head. She was two months pregnant when they killed Papa; the baby was supposed to be the thing that would balm her and bring her back, only it didn't work out that way.

Thanks be to Jah for Ras Riva Man. He knew the language of sufferation and always had ways of distracting me. He taught me how to bind his straw brooms with two strips of metal and we sold them together in the market at Brown's Town. On Saturdays, Mama let him take me with him. I sat on the crossbar of the bicycle while he balanced his brooms on one shoulder.

"Mine you don't kill my one-daughter," Mama always called. But we would be off down the road, the ends of my headscarf streaming behind. I loved the market: the noise and the cuss-cuss, the snow cones with red syrup, the smell of overripe mango and the fat woman with three bellies who sold spice and called me, "Miss Nice."

But one Saturday when he came for me, I had a mind to stay home. I loved to read like Mama, and a new girl at school had given me a book on Egyptian mummies, which I couldn't wait to devour. I did not know it would be the day the strange six-finger woman with straw hat and skirt to the ground would appear at the door and come to take Mama and the baby born too-still. When the baby was pulled from between Mama's legs, not even the mid-wife saw the woman, but I did. She was standing next to the bed fanning Mama with a banana leaf and saying, "Never mind, never mind." The baby was small and blue like a bit of night sky and the midwife sucked in her breath and put the infant in a plastic basin at the foot of the bed and covered it with a white cloth. Then she sucked in her breath again and began stuffing rags between Mama's legs. The room smelled of bay rum and Vicks vapour rub. The six-finger woman motioned to Mama, "Come," but Mama held up a finger as if to say, "Not yet." Then she called me to her side, reached for a paradise plum in a bag on the bedside table, and put it in my mouth. I knew that every strong and everlasting thing she felt for me was in that sweet.

"Jah live," she said, and closed her eyes.

The plum melted in my mouth as the six-finger woman reached into my mother's chest, pulled out a tiny dragon-fly and released it through the window.

"Mama!" I called, but her breath was fly gone.

The mid-wife was rubbing Mama down with Limacol and had not seen a thing. "Oh God, oh JesusGod," she said, when she finally saw that Mama was not breathing anymore.

I ran inside the next room to find the piece of loc Mama had given me, back when the house burned down. I pulled out all the draws, emptied boxes under the bed. *Mama!* But couldn't find it nowhere. The loc with her voice inside of it. *How could I lose it?* I hated myself. Mama lay on the bed with her hand over her heart. *Come back, Mama! Come back!* But the midwife wouldn't let me near her. I watched from the doorway as she covered the dressing table mirror with a sheet.

I'm sorry.
I'm sorry.
I'm sorry I lost the loc, Mama.

Later, Riva Man swept the four corners of the room with a new broom and drew the curtains, and shut the door. It was 1966, the year Haile Selassie I visited Jamaica. After the funeral, because I needed a respite from grieving, Riva Man took me on the bus to the airport in Kingston to see the emperor disembark from his imperial jet plane.

BACKGROUND SINGER SOUND SISTREN
[SISTAH DAWN]

Track 8.0: The Workings of His Majesty

Hear me, you think that 1966 visit was just for so? For the Most High looked to Jamaica Rasta and said to himself, "What a way these people love me. Not even my own people in Ethiopia show such honour as this, for even within the palace gates, even within the holy of holies of Addis Ababa, I have to be watchful of Judas and his pomegranate kiss." Now this is a secret known to few, and certainly no one in Jamaica, but long before his arrival, the Most High sent out a scout, scouring the island from hill to gully. The Most High sought for a locs-man of ordinary vocation, a man of sorrows and acquainted with grief, a man humble in his ways, a man who would follow his Most High and serve him with true livication. For even in Ethiopia, the Most High was a man who took no chances, picking his confidantes with a careful stick like searching soon-ripe julie mango from a tree.

And so it came to pass that Riva Man was the one chosen by Jah. At first no one missed him—he was given to going off into the bush for contemplation; only mongoose and rat-bat would know his whereabouts. But then one day someone said, But wait, is where that Rasta who used to sell the brooms-them out by St. Ann's Bay? The question fell into the river; rippled for a while before vanishing without a trace.

The truth, of course, is that Riva Man returned with the

Most High, an honoured servant, all the way to Ethiopia. For when the scout came to him in the middle night, bearing the seal of the Conquering Lion of the Tribe of Judah, Riva Man dropped the broom he was making and said three words and three words only: *Here am I.* Next week, the consulate quick-time signed papers and they dressed him up nice like an Ethiopian, and took him through customs with the rest of the Emperor's entourage, and nobody in St. Ann, in the little district of Priory, ever knew a single thing. The half has never yet been told.

Nowadays, if you go to Shashamane looking for Riva, you will not find him. And if you go to the market in Addis Ababa or Harar or Nazret, you will still not find him. Even if you go to the resting place of the Emperor's small white bones, bearing rum and incense and frangipani flowers, you will notice many things, but there will be no sign of Riva. You will find Riva, instead, in a cave in Debre Damo, smoking wisdom weed and counting the rings he makes with the smoke. *Jah live, Jah live, Jah live.*

LEENAH

Lion-Man Appears in the Sky

It was lion rain falling the day me and Riva Man went to see the emperor at the Palisadoes airport. The sky opened up and the rain came down with a mighty roar, but Riva said not to worry, Jah just cleansing the earth before he stepfoot on it. He expressed all of this with a glory of deafdread, his fingers new as rainwater. And he was right—the moment Jah iron-bird appeared in the sky, the heavens closed and the rain ceased.

A huge crowd had come to greet H.I.M. They came with flags and with drums, with thirst and with hunger, with dreadfullness and hearts out of order, with empty pockets and hundred year disappointment. They came with love and raspect, in fullticipation of Jah majesty.

H.I.M. appeared at the plane's doorway, a small man in khaki uniform. There was a dog at his side. The crowd could not contain itself; each person united in praises, it surged together, "Rastafari!" I held Riva's hand tight and Mama's words leaped from my throat, Jah live! Jah live! Jah live! For there was a feeling that Mama was alive inside of me, pressing me on. The Judah-lion held up his hand and my scalp tingled, each hair on my head numbered. Afterwards, a man in the crowd said, "Every Rasta locs grow highah today." Outside in the charged air, I walked straight-backed, my hair wrapped tall, carrying the ark of Jah-Jah covenant on my head. That would be the last time, for a long time, I held my head Sheba that way.

From the airport, Riva Man took me to my uncle Wilson's house in August Town because Uncle was my only flesh and blood and it had been decided that he should care for me now. Uncle Wilson was my father's brother. Short and bulla-faced, he did not look like Papa—they were both cut from different flour bag. Uncle was a member of Mt. Ephraim Pentecostal Church; he wore suits on Sundays and spoke in tongues and went to the barber every other Friday. He meant well, but I knew he did not approve of the way my parents had raised me. And here now was Riva with his wrap-head and bead necklaces and shirt out of his pants, like Papa.

It wasn't until he stood by the gate, ready to leave, that Riva Man explained to me that he was going to Africa. He pointed to the red continent on his shirt; he was leaving on a plane. I started to cry and he took my hand and studied my palm as if he was looking for something to soothe me. Finally he broke into a smile and pointed to a thin line under my forefinger. I was twelve years old and didn't ask what it meant, but knew that my hand-middle held something special. It was getting late and Uncle came and stood in the doorway. I put my hand on the red Africa and said goodbye. After that night, I never saw Riva Man again.

HERE-SO; HALF WAY TREE

The First Morning

Bob awakes in the clock tower the next morning. It is early but the street is already astir with vendors beginning to set out their sweets and made-in-china things. He sits up and leans against the wall, his arms and legs heavy. He slips out of the clock with no one noticing, except a girl reading a book at the bus-stop.

In the shadow of a tamarind tree behind a bar, Bob takes off his clothes and examines his body in the yellow daylight. He finds himself tall and muscular, his arms long as if built for flight. His penis is dark and shrivelled; he takes it out and pees at the base of the tree, then shakes it gingerly, aware of holding another man's member. There are no lines on his palms, no past and no future. The red headscarf falls to the ground and he is pleased, praise Jah, to discover that he is in fact a locsman; the dreads alive with a little spliff tucked inside. It is already high sun when he puts his clothes back on, wondering what to do. He empties the canvas bag—no money, only the set of keys, the container of shoe polish and stiff brush, a radio with no batteries, a bottle of Kananga water, and an old ledger book. Rhaatid. He will walk back to 56 Hope Road again, scour all of Kingston until someone recognizes him to raas—Rita, one of his children, his lawyer, his manager, one of his babymother, one of the breddren.

Rita is pulling out of the driveway when he arrives. He rushes in front of the car and blocks her way; she throws a fit, and for two long seconds all is slow motion, Rita beautiful in her rage, her nostrils flared like a passion flower. But the car pushes forward and in one quick motion Bob leaps onto the hood, presses his hands hard against the glass to show that—Jah be judge—there are no lines on his palms.

Rita screams; two men grab Bob and pull him away. She speeds down the road. Later, she will remember the palms with no lines, but only in a dream dreamed close to half light. In this dream, she says, "But I know you," and he says, "Eat jelly coconut with me tonight in the clock at Half Way Tree." All day she sings background without ceasing.

Jah live.

A prophet is never recognized in his own country, especially when that country has fallen into the mouths of dragons. Bob waves to a woman in a BMW across the street. It's his lawyer, Christine. "Is me, Bob!" She closes the tinted windows and weaves through traffic. There was a time when BMW stood for Bob Marley and the Wailers. He thinks of the foolishness of that now.

He returns to the park, searching for the boy from the night before. He wants to shine his shoes again, to see the light in his eyes from Africa reflected there. In the daylight, the park is different from how he remembered it, but the boy's tree still leans, and there's a man selling peanuts and asham.

"You see the little youth that sleep inna the park?"

"Which one?"

"The one with the play-play guitar."

"Oh, me remember him. Him in juvenile detention! Is a bad youth."

"No. Me see him last night."

"Him kill a Chinie man in August town. Man-slaughter."

It doesn't make sense. Bob has a feeling that he has stepped into the middle of someone's dream. The fall-down skin itches and there is a dull pain behind his eyes. An idea comes to him.

"You know Bob Marley?"

"Yeah?"

"What if me tell you him come back?"

"Yu mad like. Mind I don't call Bellevue Madhouse on you. Move!"

"Just listen me, nuh? Is me, Bob. Bob Marley."

"Reel out a tune fi me." The man laughs and leans back against the wall.

Bob sings a familiar chorus, but the sound that comes out is like scratched vinyl.

"Move!" the man says. And this time there is fear in his eyes.

The prophet holds up his arms and backs away, crossing the street with the flow of pedestrians.

On the other side, three brethren are reasoning outside Aquarius Recording Studio:

"As far as I&I concern, is Marcus Garvey the first Rastafari," says the long-beard one.

"Garvey prophesy and pave the path, but him was not Rasta," says the one with the yellow tam. "Garvey say, Look to Africa for the crowning of a black king. Him prophesy His Imperial Majesty, Haile I, but that don't make him Rasta."

"Rasta is a mysterious thing, is a thing of the heart. Some people Rasta and them don't even know them is Rasta." The short one eats a tangerine.

"Can a man deny His Imperial Majesty and still be Rasta?"

"Not even His Majesty-self admit he is Jah."

"And what is the meaning of Jah to I&I?"

Bob pauses at the curb. "*Haile Selassie/is the chapel*," he sings.

Taken aback by the scratched voice, the three men turn and stare at the tall-tall Ras with the brass Africas.

"*Haile Selassie/is the chapel/All the world/should know*—And a cathedral too. Selassie is cathedral too," Bob says.

"Yes-I," the breddren say together, dread-awe and one accord, watching the percussion earrings.

Bob keeps on walking down the road. He stops at a corner, still singing in scratched vinyl. *I search and I search/Sacred book of life.* A small group of children gather to hear the madman sing.

"Is a radio him have in him throat," says one.

"No, him hiding it in him shirt pocket. Is a mime, but the song scratch."

The bus comes and they all leave; Bob misses their little voices, the way he misses the boy, and misses his children. Would his children know him now? A girl looks out from the bus window. She smiles a shy smile as the bus takes off.

FROM THE ANGEL'S LEDGER BOOK

[Nutmeg on a Rusty Grater]

The street children in Kingston dance in and out of traffic, cleaning windshields. The wipers swing back and forth, but the tinted windows stay shut.

Two children on Spanish Town Road grieve for the goat drowned at the bottom of a gully. Late at night when the yard sleeps, their mother pulls the goat by its beard, skins its flesh with a sharp blade. She pares ram liver and places a slither beneath her tongue, seasons the rest with salt and yellow curry, garlic and thyme. In bed, her sheets smell of goat skin and forgotten skellion.

At Children's Hospital, all the babies in Ward 13 are crying. The angel rings a bell, but they do not stop. The crying ricochets to 1766 and back, makes a wind-devil under the big cotton tree.

In a Kingston yard, children filled with sugar-water beat a drum of goat's skin. The riddim seeps underearth, runs east and stops at a crossroads where it shifts the minute hand of a clock.

At the corner—a deaf man. He reminds of Leenah—the way he holds his finger and makes an arc in the sky. It's getting late, Bob understands. The clock does not work. He walks Half Way Tree to Crossroads, then all the way to down town. Someone has painted his face on a storefront—he holds a mic, his locs flying west. Two children lean against the mural. The girl rubs her back against it, and the boy says to Bob, "She have ringworm," then he reaches for the painted mic on the wall. "Is me the next Bob Marley," he says. "When I turn the next Bob Marley I won't hungry no more."

"You think Bob Marley never hungry?" says the girl.

"Him was a prophet, my moddah say that," says the boy. "God cast him bread on the water."

Bob takes the bottle of kananga out of his satchel and hands it to the girl. She opens the top and smells it.

"It smell like obeah perfume," she says. "But me like it."

She rubs some on her arms, then thinks better and flicks the rest at Bob's face. The boy takes the bottle and flicks at Bob too. They both giggle and Bob jumps, playing dandy-shandy with the drops; kananga wets his cheeks.

"Save some for my back!" the girl says.

As Bob leaves, she takes a pencil and draws little circles on the mural. "Bob Marley have ringworm," she says.

The worm in her voice follows Bob as he walks with no rhyme or reason, still testing his new legs.

Backstage at Ward Theatre a group prepares to rehearse *River Mumma and the Golden Table*. No one sees Bob slip in in the shadows. It is cool inside and he slips down into a velvety chair, leans back and closes his eyes, imagines his seat sinking into dark matter, all the way to a home-sweet-home lamp. The room smells faintly of sweat and talcum powder. He remains in that drowsy-between as someone rearranges props; there are feet up and down, and voices. In the dream-distance, his mother shouts, Nesta! Calling him by his old name. She holds a cup of warm milk and stands in a doorway. She is robust from yellow yam and dasheen.

Lights. He wakes up.

On stage, the blue lamps are bright. The actor-boy, Sweet Mouth, wants to find a golden table. It is buried under a river at the bottom of a cotton tree. He steps tip-toe into the water in knee-high socks, watching for duppy. Bob laughs and everyone turns around; the rehearsal stops. Someone escorts him outside; he looks left then right; heads back to Half Way Tree.

FROM THE ANGEL'S LEDGER BOOK

[Seed Fall]

"A very pleasant and interesting ceremony took place at Halfway Tree market yesterday afternoon when, on the invitation of the chairman of the St. Andrew Parochial Board, His Excellency the Acting Governor planted a tree to take the place of the historic cotton tree, which had to be cut down in connection with the building of the Memorial Clock Tower in the capital of St. Andrew."
—February 27, 1913—The Gleaner.

"It [the West Indian cotton tree] hath very large roots and spredeth at the spurs with cavities, soe that men may stand there as behind the arches and great supporting pillars in churches and stately structuers."—John Taylor writes this with his feather pen in 1687.

December 31, 1766—A young boy is hanged at the big cotton tree. Sundays, while master and family were at church, he played the black keys of the house piano, picking out rebellion—the sound so wail-and-war, it riled up the people, made them remember their true names. Now they have put turn-luck in the master's water. The sugar cane is withered and the overseer has a fever that will not leave. Seven men and three women have escaped to the hills. There is a word—

January 30, 1832—Moonshine, and two make love under the great silk cotton at Half Way Tree; they embrace in the crook of a root, soft-soft pods fallen all around. They must leave early morning; mistress must not know. Later, when their tongues touch, they feel a word rise up, an ancient word, forgotten—

The silk cottons on this island converse underground. There is a language sent via rootways; it sounds like this / / To destroy a cotton tree is to disrupt a long-time discourse.

February 03, 1832—Two slaves are whipped under the great ceiba at Half Way Tree: runaway lovers. The angel is there when the woman's child miscarries. Her wail ricochets blood-red, into the yet-to-come.

Ceiba: Taino. The mango came from India, the breadfruit from Tahiti, and ackee from W. Africa, but on this island, the ceiba/silk cotton lived from the beginning.

Rain day, 1509—The angel is there when a Taino girl hides under the great ceiba. On the run from a Spanish soldier, she crouches in the twist of a root and he does not find her.

Tea of ceiba, bark and leaf—good for venereal disease and urinary tract infection. The people learn this.

In another country, the great ceiba marks the centre of wheel-and-come. One cycle ends here and a new one begins.

Woe Day, Woe Day, Year of Forgetfulness—A woman watches workers cut down the tree to make way for the clock. A limb breaks, and her gasp sounds all the way back in time-ago where a boy with a noose—

Light as spirit laugh, the wood is both coffin and cricket bat. The wise ones sprinkle rum before they set out in ceiba canoe.

April 21, 1966—This year is the 200th anniversary of the murder of the ancestor at the great silk cotton at Half Way Tree. No one knows this. Business as usual.

And this day, too, is the day His Imperial Majesty, Haile I of Ethiopia arrives in Jamaica; his small feet touch the ground.

Later, back at Half Way Tree, Bob fumbles for the keys to the clock tower. He slips in quickly and closes the door, lights the spliff that has been hidden in the depths of his hair. He needs to think. Sliding down against the wall, he closes his eyes and takes in the smoke. There is a little space under the eaves where a bird has made her nest. The smoke fills her lungs and she dozes off feeling warm and languid.

The tower was built in 1913 in memory of King Edward VII. King Edward visited Jamaica once, a long time ago, to fulfill a last request of his mother, Queen Victoria. Touring Kingston, he was accompanied by his wife, Alexandra, and the Governor General; and when his carriage paused by the old cotton tree—where the clock tower would later stand—he stroked his beard, admired the nesting birds and thought it a nice respite. No one even knew he had had that thought, but when he died and the grand tree was cut down so the tower could go up in his name, his ghost crossed sea in an Atlantic steamer and took up residence in the clock tower. The clock had four faces, facing the four directions, and King Edward's ghost liked to turn the hands for passersby. On the day in August 1962, when Jamaica received independence from Britain, King Edward's ghost, drunk with whisky, fell to the floor. *I am/ Thou art/You are/He is/We are/Ye are/You are/They are*, he sang. That's when a duppy slave boy, murdered at the cotton tree, reached up into the tower and spun the steel wheels around and around. He spun with such intent, he turned back time all the way to 1766, for two whole seconds—long enough to dance one more beat, and try, try to retrieve the word at the tip of his tongue, the crowd marvelling at his lynch-step feet—but it was too late. Back in the tower, he took a sniff of King Edward's whisky, then disappeared in the Kingston heat. Few know that this is the real reason the clock at Half Way Tree did not work for many years.

Tonight, as Bob smokes his spliff, he hears a clinking sound, this time of ice in a glass.

"Is who?" Bob calls.

There is a long silence and then a cube falls to the ground.

Bob pulls at his spliff and closes his eyes and when he opens them again there is a man with a big belly and a bushy white beard crouched in the opposite corner.

Bob studies him for a while, then breaks into a smile.

"Is you them call Faadah Deadmas?"

"Your Majesty, for you."

The bird stirs in her nest and Bob blows a little smoke up to the rafters.

"Is only one King I rate."

Edward raises an eyebrow.

"The King of Kings, Lord of Lords, Elect of God, the Conquering Lion of the Tribe of Judah, His Imperial Majesty, Haile Selassie I of Ethiopia, the Most High, Jah Rastafari."

"Well, that's a mouthful," Edward says.

"Is H.I.M. I rate."

There is another silence and then Bob holds out his hand.

"Them call me, Bob. Bob Marley," he says.

They stay there for a while, Bob smoking his spliff, Edward coughing and sighing. And then because the English king seems so forlorn and despicable trapped there in the clock tower with his whisky, Bob finds himself saying, "My father was an Englishman."

King Edward puts down his glass and shifts his legs. Bob inhales the last of the herb.

RASTAMAN

Three Legged Horse: Bob Marley Speaks

I&I never really know my faadah. Him run-way, leave me when me was just a youth. Little white man with narrow shoulders. You know that cancer that was in mi foot? I believe is a white man cancer. You see how life funny? Is cause-a my faadah, Norval Marley, the English man who abandon me, why mi foot did sore. That's what me know.

Me see a photo of mi faadah high up on a horse. Him wearing a hat. And his foot in the stirrup. People say all you had to do was blow on him and his two eyes spill over; he was a cry-cry man. Bet him would hear that little bird up in this clock and start cry over it, just like that. But don't let that fool you. Only a coward throw away his son in the street. Coward is coward. Check this. One day him take me to town and drop me off at an ole woman house, give me a sideways look and dodge through the gate. The ole woman see he nah come back and she give me a cot at her bed-foot. After she fall sleep, me hide under the stink pillow and cry eye-water just like mi small-back, pussy-heart so-called faadah. That night me hate him so till. Me hate him! The back of him head and the white shirt— that was the last me see of him. Wouldn't even fight for me to raas.

From that, every night me hear him gallop in mi sleep. Gallop gallop. Sometimes it rain and even the rain sound like horse a gallop. Horse hoof pounding the yard. Hear this, the horse in my dream have three legs and one night me run after the horse and catch him and wrestle with him. The horse rear up on the two back legs-them, but me grab onto the front one and me hold mi ground and don't let go.

Me want know why my faadah throw me away like that, and me cry out in mi sleep, "Why?" The three-legged horse pulling away from me, but me keep mi two foot on the ground and me don't let go.

Every night for three years, me wrestle with that man on that three-leg horse and one night I decide to give him back him name, and when I open my mouth to give it back, the horse get way and gallop a bush.

But hear me now, I get to realize I-man never need that rider on that three-legged horse because I&I have only one faadah and that faadah is the Conquering Lion of the Tribe of Judah, Haile Selassie I, Jah Rastafari.

Is him I rate.

FROM BLOODFIAH, RECORD OF DREAMSLOST

Track 17.0: The Queen of Sheba: She Who Parts Her Hoof
[Version]

There is a story that goes this way: after her visit to the land of Israel, the Queen of Sheba missed her hoof and wrestled with a horse in her dream. She wrestled thirty nights with this horse. "Give me your hoof," she said, but the horse would not give in. On the last night, she tore off the horse's hoof and tried it on for size, but because it was not cloven, it would not fit. Meanwhile, the horse—now three-legged—escaped and leaped through the bottom of the queen's dream, galloping to a boy thousands of years away fighting injustice in his sleep.

Just before morning, a goat came leaping in the horse's stead and, at the smell of her salt-water sorrow, wrenched off its hoof and gave it to the queen. Makeda danced with the goat's hoof until early morning and when she awoke, she felt a new peace. She kissed her baby asleep in his cradle, pleased that she had righted the hoof, albeit in a dream. This, they say, is how Queen Makeda made peace with the connivings of Solomon.

Jah bless.

Bob had waited a long time to utter those words, rehearsed them over and over as a child. "Me hated him for not coming back." And now, here after his own death, in the clock tower at Half Way Tree, standing in another man's skin, he is having his say before an old English king.

King Edward takes another sip of his whisky. "A good drink helps with many a trouble," he says, and disappears.

Bob hears the ice in his glass; every now and then a cube falls and melts on the floor. He has gone all day without eating and is beginning to feel faint. He empties the canvas bag again. He needs some money. Maybe he can sell the radio or the wooden cane. It is old but well-made, intricate in design. He can sell it at the craft market downtown. Then the thought comes to him to turn out his pockets. They are all empty, except for one—something wrapped in a piece of toilet paper. He sits down in the centre of the clock tower, unwraps the tissue and finds a gold ring engraved with a lion. He still has no remembrance of why he has returned and does not recognize the ring at all, but at sight of the imperial lion, his eyes fill with tears. Taking it as a sign from the Almighty, he praises Jah who in his great lovefulness has sent a ring with his own seal, so his son can buy a plate of food.

*Missed Gate: Many Are Called but Few Are Chosen; or, Revelation of
Wisdom According to Jah Prophets (1:07)*

(A man is sitting on a stoop by the side of the road, the angle of
his cheekbones set to catch Jah bless. Soon as you pass, he pulls
something from his pocket.

"You with the nice shoes. Stop here," he says. Usually, you hold
your head straight and just keep walking, but something about the
Kingston 12 in his voice slows down your feet.

"Two patty and a box drink, and the ring is yours," he says. It's
a lion of Judah ring—black onyx with the dandy one in gold. You
have seen those rings before; replicas of Bob's ring are already everywhere. A jeweller in Brooklyn sells nice ones for seventy-five
dollars. In London, for fifty pounds. A friend of yours wears one
on his middle finger. In Addis Ababa such rings have always been
common as lies. In any event, you do love lions and two patties and
a box drink is not a bad price. But this is a madman and you are a
reasonable person, no true?

"Next time," you say, and keep on going. As you leave, the man
bursts into psalm, *Awake Zion, Awake*. The voice pulls at your tail-
bone, but you hold your back straight and do not look back.)

DUB-SIDE CHANTING

Track 18.0: The Uprising of Fall-down

Fall-down finds the Prophet's clothes folded at the bottom of Studio D. The beautiful woman gone, he puts the clothes on, wondering at the marvels of redgreengold underpants in 100% cotton. Still, he misses his Africas' clink-clink at his ears and the wooden staff which he had made with his own two hands. He runs his fingers over his smooth scalp. What a bad-luckyness to be in Bob's skin but have a baldhead.

H.I.M. is fishing from a bridge by a quiet river, a dog curled asleep at his heels. It jumps up, barking as Fall-down approaches.

"Lulu!" H.I.M. calls. The dog stops, one ear pricked up, the other down. Both dog and master waiting.

Fall-down has not thought what he ought to say, and the words which fall from his mouth surprise him.

"I was there when you tried on Empress Menen's pointed-toe shoes," he says.

At these words, H.I.M. is transported to a March day shortly after his marriage when he and the empress had frolicked behind the closed doors of their bedchamber like two young lions on the red satin eiderdown. He had lost some foolish bet or other and for that she made him try on her pointed-toe Italian slippers, she laughing on the floor.

"I was there when you cleaned the she-lion with your tongue," Fall-down says, for the words are streaming out of him now and he cannot stop them.

"What fallen-angel speaks to an emperor like that?" The twinkle is gone from H.I.M.'s eye.

"And I made the pet lions in the garden roar at the conception of each of your seven children."

At mention of the lions H.I.M. laughs, then becomes quiet. He had loved his lions, but after the coup, Mengistu threw them into the Addis Ababa Zoo to teach them a lesson.

"I was there when you invited the maid into your bed chamber," Fall-down says. The smile on H.I.M.'s face disappears.

"Ça suffit!"

The emperor has always been wont to speak French when annoyed. Lulu begins yapping around Fall-down's feet. Fall-down backs away, his arms raised.

"Is me, Negus," he says to the little Chihuahua. "You don't remember—"

The dog stops barking and Fall-down puts his hand over his mouth to stop the words. H.I.M. kisses his teeth, tsk, and keeps on fishing.

It is evening and the nutmeg tree is quiet. If he stays still, Fall-down can hear the hum of Hector's sewing machine, the sound distinct though untraceable. Still, he is eager to locate the source. H.I.M.'s dog trots behind, sniffing the ground. The slope is steep and wet and Fall-down trips in Bob's small boots. He tries to rise, but each time stumbles back—into a patch of wild sea-cloud flowers. He feels as if he is drowning, looks for something to grab onto and finding nothing, slides again into the mass of blue-blue.

"No mind. I used to falling," he says to the dog, "Last time was because I love a girl; she—"

"Ça suffit!" H.I.M. says. He is standing at the edge of the field. Lulu wags her tail and runs to her companion and Fall-down is not sure whether the Judah lion spoke to Lulu or to him. He decides to hold his tongue, just the same.

"Bob call for me plain as day," he says instead, "right in the middle of Half Way Tree."

Lulu sniffs around Fall-down's shoes, then squats and pees on his feet.

"The prophet was convinced he still needed the ring," says H.I.M. "Some souls, even great ones, do not learn right away."

Lulu's warm pee trickles in the fallen angel's shoe, and he remembers—the ring had been left in his trouser pocket.

STUDIO Z
HECTOR

Track 13.5: Of Zion and Ships and High Seas

Hector salutes like a captain, then keeps on sewing. He pedals away, conversing with the beautiful black Singer. His house is filled with cerulean blue suits of every description. They bulge out of closets and are stacked onto shelves; hooked to nails on the wall and on hangers swinging from the rafters. One bed is piled so high with cerulean blue that the suits touch the ceiling. "I know where Zion is," he says.

HERE-SO; HALF WAY TREE

Second Morning; Dubwise Outside Aquarius

Next morning there is riddim from all four directions. To the west towards Hagley Park, a street-corner evangelist ti-tings her tambourine. A man beside her speaks in tongues. He is describing sweet Beulah land. A place that can only be revealed in the tongues of angels. To the east, coming down from Hope Road, Bob recognizes the voice of the Upsetter on the car stereo, a new tune he hasn't heard before. And to the north, at the traffic light, his own voice on a bicycle boom box, moving Jah people.

But underneath these voices, there is a deep bass dub coming up from the south. The bass so deep it stirs old cotton tree roots underground. A girl reading a book at the bus stop feels the riddim in her loins. She stops and looks down the road, turns the corner of a page to mark the beat. Bob feels it too, dubwise. He follows the ground/bone/base/rock/pulsefull sound, weaving past schoolchildren, a stray dog and a youth selling Jesus slippers, straight to the reverb of thunderclap and three Rastas—this time different ones—reasoning outside the Aquarius Record Shop. Rain. Sends them under the piazza for cover.

"*You can ride a chord to that place. That holy place. Deep is the riff of Jah-Jah majesty. The dubside is the spirit side,*" chants the one with the white tam.

"Which is more powerful, the lion or the lamb?"

"The lion is the lamb dormant."

"Yes-I."

"The lamb is the message incarnate."

"Yes-I."

"Listen breddren, the lion stand before the lamb. But the lamb is the greater."

"Yes-I."

"I go National Arena and hear Bob roar like a lion. When him open him mouth, him have two-row teeth and is a roar come out."

Music is a mystic ting, chants the white tam Rasta.

"Why bring Bob inna dis? Bob was a man of the flesh like you and me."

"Him was a prophet, Rasta. A lion-prophet."

"The only true lion is Haile-I. The scripture declare the glory of His Imperial Majesty."

We are the lions of Judah. Don't let anyone fool-ya.

"Is Bob I talking bout."

"Mine you look to the man instead the message," Bob says.

Just like the day before, they all turn and look at him.

"The next prophet will come as a lamb unto us," says the short one.

"Mine you miss him."

"*And the she-lion, she rising*," sings the Rasta, watching a girl coming towards them. She holds a book gilded as scripture. Her hips move deep bass, the way riverstones move water.

"A prophet is never honoured in his own country," Bob says.

The Rasta with the white tam looks deep into Bob's eyes. His eyebrows fan in the middle like sacred dark ferns.

Holy holy is the lamb, he chants and passes the spliff.

The girl walks past them; her elbow brushes against Bob's sleeve. A bougainvillea flutters out of her book.

FROM THE ANGEL'S LEDGER BOOK

[Maracas]

Release Day—Kingston 11, "Concrete Dub." King Tubby feels it.

The bass rhythm of this island massages the earth's structure. Vibrates rock underground. Quickens bones of the departed.

Twelve high school girls wait at a bus stop in front of Holy Cross Church. The liturgy of laughter over one-drop beat.

Down below, a dead woman's hip-bone remembers. Dust shifts in the hollow of pelvis.

September, 1978—The angel is in love with Bob Marley's woman. The head of her woman serpent rises.

May, 1981—An uncommon spider ropes a story in the rafters of the clock tower at Half Way Tree.

HERE-SO; HALF WAY TREE

Hum

Here it is, late into the second day, and Bob still cannot remember why he has returned. Already, he wants to *get outta this structure; is a Alice in Wonderdread bodysuit this to rah. And mi shoulder blades—them heavy; like them don't fix right.* Somewhere on the Dub-side, a nutmeg tree waits on a quiet hill; he longs to light a spliff there and sit and reason at the right hand of Jah. But how to find the way back? There is something he must do first, this much he knows—find an undisclosed gate. *Your heart will tell you where it is.*

Still, there is not a soul to turn to. "Is me, Bob," he says to people who know him. They slam the door or laugh in his face. He walks around Kingston, pausing at each wrought-iron gate, wondering at the fanciful designs—sunburst, Anancy rope, stepping stone. He sees one with a star of Haile-I that makes him stop and touch all six of its points, put his hand through the centre and feel the air on the other side. There is a sign, *Beware of Bad Dog.* Rhaatid. He could catch a ride to country, but something tells him to stay here-so—in Half Way Tree. There is something about the clock, this ugly, Babylon clock that never tell the right time that keeps him here. He thinks of Leenah. Would she recognize him? Leenah always saw soul-deep, not skin-deep.

It is afternoon by the time he gets to Mona. Miss Ivy does not recognize him either. She looks him up and down, stands a safe distance and does not open her gate. The iron is black spiral and latched with a padlock. Leenah is not there and Miss Ivy doesn't know where she is.

"Last thing I know she had a baby," she says. A little girl that cry with her mouth closed—make it sound like a hum. "Is you the father?"

Bob hums a tune as he walks back to Half Way Tree. *Jah Jah dawta/ Zion come*—his children would like that tune. He hums it over and over, testing the limits of his fall-down voice. It is a new instrument, even scratch-up as it is, and he might as well play it. He hits a deep chord and the sound vibrates in his foot-bottom. He walks all the way to Balmoral Ave., massaging sound under his feet. At Crossroads, he hits another chord and the hum fills his structure, reggae in *a capella*, a whole sound system in his throat. When harmony enters his locs, his feet levitate above the concrete—just enough to make him trip in the effort to find ground. *Who the hell is this raas angel?*

He sits on a wall, takes the book from his satchel. A small book, but heavy-so. And the pages brown like someone soak each in pimento and old rum. The handwriting is at first illegible, the movement of absent-minded black ants across a page. But then his eyes adjust, and he sees—the dark ink, beautiful in its meandering, made clear. He turns a page at random. The words written in bass with tenor layered on top; sometimes a faint soprano seeping through.

FROM THE ANGEL'S LEDGER BOOK

[Fende]

May 24, 1976—A naked woman wrapped in cellophane faces the clock at Half Way Tree. She recites words so ancient, they are almost unspeakable. Every now and then, she has to stop and look for a syllable in the sky.

Her name is Beul, but no one knows this, not even she. She attends the spot where the old cotton tree once grew.

The hands of the clock wait at 7:05. It is the longest minute in history.

August 14, 1977—The women on this island walk as though their hips are the pulse of the Milky Way. This is the real reason stars fall.

Such a walk can make even an angel wish to be human. But angels—even less experienced ones—should know better.

Still, there is a woman with a mole the shape of Africa on her thigh. And oh-when-she-walks—

There is an angel who longs to kiss that mole.

At 2:37 a.m. a young cannabis sativa unfurls her blossom at the bottom of a cemetery. "Bad-ass bass," a duppy girl whispers.

Only one woman there is with a mark the shape of Africa on her thigh. Bob had craven for that sweetness too; he remembers this. But how come this raas angel know so much?

He is almost at the gas station and can see the clock tower now, a bird on top. And that's the other thing—he has extraordinary vision, but only from a distance. He'll need some light to read in the clock tower. A girl sells made-in-China flashlights at the curb. *Get your flash, flash it; hurricane flash, flash; I flash for you; nice price too for you.* A flash for a spliff, Bob says, taking a bit of herb from his hair. The girl glances at the spliff, then shines a light in Bob's eye; she catches her breath for a moment, glimpsing a thing unexpected; but then she spits on the ground and walks away. *This little light of mine,* sings a woman in front of him. He follows her all the way up the road, her grey hair tied up in cloth. Her voice reminds of his mother's when he was a boy in church, a country hillside pitch, all strong-back and wood smoke; he needs this voice. His mother—in Miami now— would not recognize her son. But for some reason, it does not matter anymore. At the bus stop the old woman turns around, gives Bob some change then steps onto the 46/Meadowbrook. Bob opens his mouth to thank her but no sound comes out. The woman looks out through the window and smiles; her teeth are white as a young girl's.

The bus leaves and Bob opens his hand. The change is enough to buy two candles and a box of matches. Outside Aquarius the bredbren still reason the mystery of sound. JAH-JAHJAH-JAHJAH-JAH JAH-JAH goes the reverb. It's late and he crosses the street to the clock. He must enter at just the right moment, when no one is looking.

At the base of mother-ticking Babylon he sits and waits; wishing that lightning would strike down the tower and be done with it. And then there is a shout—*Blouse and skirt!*—across the street; a woman flicks open a ratchet knife and another pulls a razor from her bra. In the cuss-cuss and rah-rah palangpang, all eyes and ears are diverted in one direction. The babyfather slinks away in the shadows. Bob opens the door and slips quickly inside.

FROM THE ANGEL'S LEDGER BOOK

[Bells on a Girl's Ankle Bracelet]

March 11, 1977—The angel, Negus, enters the bedroom of Mr. and Mrs. W. on Maxfield Ave. Mrs. W. catches a whiff of the angel's scent and is immediately aroused. Mr. W. never knows a thing.

March 23, 1977—The angel, Negus, assists at the conception of girl twins. The sound of double fertilization is like bells on a girl's ankle bracelet.

March 25, 1977—The angel, Negus, blows the woman-Lara with breath of a male lion. Neither she nor the babyfather know the true reason she calls Jah name.

Reminder to self: Angels of Desire work with the seven senses of titillation, creating the conditions for humans to enjoy each other. An Angel of Desire must never physically touch or copulate with humans.

And such angels must never leave incriminating evidence.

It's late and the words have returned to black ants on the page. Bob's shoulder blades are sore; he hates this dry skin, this clock. A she-spider watches from the corner. *You have two club-foot but at least there is no melanoma to rah.* He thinks she says that. He blows out the candle and when he falls asleep, he meets Leenah in his dream. She shows him her Africa, but won't let him touch it. Tell me my true name, he says. It is a name without syllable, she replies.

LEENAH

Of Swallowtails

I have a recurring dream of two lions side by side. I pass between them and they roar, but do not harm me. I love dreaming. In my dreams I can *hear*. I hear music and the dj on the radio, and my mother calling my name and Bob saying, *Let me see yuh Africa. How far up yuh leg it is? It touch yuh panty?*

In my dreams, only Anjahla is silent. I see her mouth moving but no sound comes out. Her lips say, *Mama*. I want to hear Anjahla in my dream. In my dream I say, *Talk louder Anjahla! Let me hear you.* And I see Anjahla's mouth go, *Mama! You can hear me now? I sound like a swallowtail butterfly, Mama. Did you know they are the largest butterflies in Jamaica? And they are almost extinct. I read it in a book.*

And there's this too—us shelling peas together last week:

"I want to sing a song only fish and creatures in the deep-deep can hear," Anjahla says.

"And where does that come from?"

"Just something I feel—"

She looks out the window, as if counting the raindrops.

"I read in a book that whales sing to each other. Do you think mother whales sing to their young?"

"Maybe," I say.

"And do the young sing back?"

I laugh. But she is serious.

"I am going to sing a whale song so high-high that it goes low-low," she says.

Light moves across her eyes like a film flicking by.

"That's nice," I say. "But a girl singing like a whale would be like turning a tree into a philharmonic choir, a book into a 12-string electric guitar, an apple into Motown. Your voice can't—"

That's when Anjahla slaps me on the mouth. I am astonished. She is not a rude child; and has never acted this way.

"And why not, *Mama*?" She puts a stress on the Mama. I see it—by the way her lips make "m" twice. It is a moment I will remember for the rest of my life. And that's when I know not to hold back this child. For she is a rebel girl with a will to do; she will sing her whale song and shake her whale tail, if she wants. My Anjahla.

Edward is playing a game of solitaire up on the ladder. A Queen of Hearts floats to the ground. Bob is tired now. He has wandered two days hoping to stumble upon the gate of return. He unwraps the ring from the toilet paper and puts it on his finger; something in the air is suddenly disturbed. There is a flutter of wings up in the rafters and Edward's cards come swirling down. The ribbon of cold air, which is Edward, pushes under the crack at the bottom of the door, then whirls down Hagley Park Road, all the way to the waterfront and out to sea, a squall transporting him, "Britanniaaaaa," to a ship just leaving the harbour.

Bob feels the troubled air; picks up the cards and stacks them in a corner. He takes off the ring, nestles it in the toilet paper and settles down for the night.

Early-early the third morning Bob gets up and cracks the door. It's raining outside. All night his arms and legs and the far places of his back have itched; he's in the skin of a frienemey. Quick, he dashes into the rain; the warm water soothes. He stands in the middle of Half Way Tree; his open mouth receives the water. There is a new energy in the street, something more electric; radiowaves travel the length of his locs. It is not long before the square is filled with business.

He will watch today for the gate of Jah. *Your heart will tell you where it is.* Perhaps his foot will slip and he will find it. He wants to get out of Kingston Babylon, catch a bus to Nine Mile and eat some drop-down mango; visit Omeriah's grave, but something, again, tells him he must remain in Half Way Tree, close to where the old cotton tree used to grow. The ancestor spirits love cotton trees; this is what his grandfaadah, Omeriah, used to say. They were vex that the tree was torn down to put up a Babylon clock tower. When Bob stands with his feet firm, he feels the roots of the old tree underground—the still-alive roots, extending forty feet across the street, holding communion with ancestors. And isn't this the true reason so many mad come to Half Way Tree? The lifeforce and spirits of the old cotton tree call them.

There is something else too. Bob notices that each time he awakes and steps through the clock tower door, something about Babylon has changed. The first day, all seemed as he had last remembered it—the raucous of the four directions, the hum of heat rising from concrete, the soprano of sufferation, the earth spinning on its axis like a turntable. On the second morning, something shifted, though he was not sure what. He stepped out into a new hi-fi of tribulation, made a mental note of it and headed up the road. A bobo Rasta gave him a black mango; he bit into it and praised the Most High. And this third morning, he notices something else—it is in the rhythm of the dawtah crossing the street in tight jeans and big earrings, the wonder of the little phone ringing like a sound system in her back pocket. Bob has never known a phone like that.

He follows her all the way to the post office, watches her flip the phone open as she goes inside.

"A patty and a box drink for this ring," he says when she pauses at the counter.

She licks her stamps and does not look up; the lion waits humble as a lamb in the toilet paper. In her haste to get away from Bob, she drops an envelope on the floor. He picks it up and calls after her, but she does not look back; the phone in her pocket rings again against her bottom. He stands there at the post office door, holding her letter up to the sun when there, in the upper right corner, he sees himself on the stamp—in full colour—holding a microphone, his locs flying. The stamp reads, "50th Anniversary of the Birth of Bob Marley." Fifteen years have gone by since his passing, perhaps even more.

Outside, Bob looks up and down the street, taking in the square. The clock has a fresh coat of paint. A man rides by on a bicycle, a flag with a six-pointed star blowing behind him. Across the road, an old woman smiles and waves.

"Me know you!" she calls.

"Where you know me from?"

"You is God pickney," she says.

Music blares from a youth's car stereo, fast and electric. The youth spits through the window and pushes through traffic.

"What they call this new music?" Bob shouts to the woman.

"Is dancehall—even an old lady know that."

Bob walks away; contemplates how sound has changed. He bends down and draws a star on the concrete with a piece of chalk stone, for now he overstands that each morning as he opens the door to Half Way Tree, he steps into a different year, and new era. But look the workings of Jah. He will journey the six points of the star—through years and rumours of years—all the way to the yet-to-come.

With new higherstanding, Bob walks down the road, noticing how Babylon has changed yet remained the same. In the end, Babylon is Babylon. He walks until he comes across a man with a small stall at a bus stop. He sells bottled water and bag juice. When he sees Bob, he calls, "Ras!" Bob pauses and is about to move on when he recognizes the man as the youth he saw the first day, the boy with the play-play guitar. He is older now, his head tied with a red bandana and a little ram goat beard at his chin.

"Is you that, Ras?" the man says, "when me never see you, me think them kill you to raahtid!"

"Me come back."

Then he looks at Bob hard. "So where you disappear go?"

"Inna the clock—down the street."

"Ah, Ras! Still full of jokes! Still full of jokes!" He laughs and slaps Bob's back, speaking with so much excitement little bits of spit accumulate at the corners of his mouth. "And not a year show on your face!"

"But tomorrow when me come again, you will show five more," Bob says.

Delroy laughs and slaps Bob's back again. Then he stops and says, "You still checking the girls?"

"This morning me see a dawtah with a phone in her back pocket."

"That's the Ras I know! That's the Ras I know!" Delroy says, the spit bubbling at his corner-mouth.

Bob is pleased to discover that his responses satisfy Delroy. By now he realizes that it is useless to insist on his true identity. He reaches into his satchel and pulls out a little bundle. "Two patty and a box drink, for this ring." he says.

Delroy looks at the ring with interest.

"Oh, is a Bob Marley ring!"

"Yeah?"

"Yeah-man. Bob Marley used to sport a ring like that. Everybody want one now. Where you get it?"

"In my pocket."

"But where you get it?"

"My faadah give me it."

"Ah, Ras. Mad same way! Mad same way!" He cups the ring and blows on it, then rubs it to a shine with the hem of his shirt. "Them have a jeweller downtown make these kinda Rasta ring. I bet is him do this one."

"Take it," Bob says. "Where me going me no need material tings."

"Nah?"

Delroy blows on the ring again. "Where you going?"

"Zion," Bob says.

Delroy puts the ring back in Bob's hand, then crosses the street. He comes back with a patty and a coco bread and a pineapple box drink, gives Bob a stool next to the stall.

"Keep the ring," he says. "Is your faadah give you it."

Bob eats the patty and crumples the brown bag. He is thinking of his children. A little girl with thick plaits. He misses her. Misses his nice girl. She would be grown up now; all his children grown up now. And his sons—one of them maybe about this man's age. He pictures him. Yes, standing in a doorway, eating an orange. "Daddy?"

"Where yuh faadah deh?" Bob turns to Delroy.

"How you mean? Is you my faadah," Delroy says. "Ever since that day you shine my shoes, is you my faadah. Only a faadah could shine a shoes like that. "

"Shine shoes don't make faadah. Is not me yuh faadah."

There is a flash of hurt on Delroy's face. Just a twinge—but Bob sees it.

DELROY

Birthday Cake

You see me? I know where Zion gate is. Is in a shoe brush and a can of black polish. I glimpse inside the gate already with my own two eyes. Strike me dead if is lie I telling. Zion is in the mad man shining your shoes and he shine and shine and shine so long, you forget about your mother lock up in the freezer and your baby sister mouth turning purple like periwinkle flowers and your auntie house too full to hold you. You see me? I know where Zion is. Zion is in the mad man's hands moving the brush over your feet. At first you refuse to let him to rah, but then he brushing harder and harder and you feel the bristles through the leather, your skin pricking up. His hands so strong and so powerful, he pressing down your soles till your feet start grow roots and now you don't want him stop, cause the roots growing longer, cracking the concrete, digging under ground, pass cockroach and sewage and Public Works pipe, to water and worms and earth so brown and so pretty you could slice it and eat it like a piece of cake—the kind of cake that bake only in picture book for nice little girls and boys with pointy hats on their head and their mommies and daddies clapping nearby. And all the while the mad angel brushing and brushing, the little Africas at his ears going clink-clink, clink-clink. *You see your face? You see your face yet?* And you look way down and you look again. And Africa ringing out a tune just for you. And, yes, you see your face—shiny and smiling and eating birthday cake in Zion to raas.

"Is you my faadah," Delroy says, and the thing Bob glimpses on his face reminds of an ache in the chord of a song he used to sing. The song was *I Know a Place* and the blood always rushed behind his eyes when he got to the end.

"How old you is now?"

"Twenty-four." Delroy pulls at his ram goatie. "I have a daughter—three years old. When she get big, I want you shine her shoes!"

"I would like that," Bob says, and he traces the lines on his wood staff.

"The babymother is a balm woman." A truck drives by carrying a load of chicks in crates. "I went to her yard to wash off my heart."

Delroy opens two Maltas and they sit by the side of the road, watching the sky darken.

DELROY

The Deliverance Bath

I was just a youth living in the park with the frogs and my make-believe guitar. At night, the park full of bad man; some of them had guns. I had a gun too—I find it buried under leaves one night and I keep it for myself. The gun name was Lloyd. I put it in my school bag because I wasn't going school nomore, just begging a money from the nice girls when they come out of class. Some of them give me change and some of them give me them left-over drinks. The Rastas in front Aquarius take care of me too; sometime them buy me patty and one time one of them let me hold his guitar. And I make friend with a duppy boy. I only see him once, but I know he is there—over by the clock. He have a rope around his neck, and one early morning he used the end of it to beat a man who try to steal my bag. But at night, the frogs croak and carry on and I sleep with my head on the bag and Lloyd inside of it, and when rain fall I don't have nowhere to go. The shoes—the ones the mad-angel shine—too small for me, but I cut off the back and wear them like slippers.

The rude-boys in the park, them older than me and they take me for joke: Youth, if you shoot that frog for me, I buy you a box drink. Youth-man, if you shoot that dog, I give you a money. I fraid of them so I do what they tell me. One night one of them say, Youth, hold up a shop with me tomorrow, I buy you a new pair of boot. He take me to a shop in August Town just as the Chinie-man was closing it; and I watch the door with my gun while he hold up the man and clear out the cash register. When he done, he make the man stretch out on the ground like Jesus on the cross and he shoot him in his two hand-middle and in his feet and in his side. I see the whole thing. Is me the Chinie-man eyes rest on before him dead. Next day, he take me to Sammy's and he buy me a new pair of shoes, just like he promise, but I never enjoy those shoes. Those shoes never bless. Those shoes torment me more than the frogs at night and the mosquito in the bush. Every night I dream-see the Chinie-man on the cross.

Church couldn't help me; the church people too clean-and-shave-and-powder-up to rhaatid and I was a dutty streggae bwoy. Is only my little play-play guitar see me through, and the music coming from across the street, and the remembrance of the mad-angel shining my shoes like my feet was the only feet in the world. When them send me go juvenile detention, is that remembrance save me—me, looking down on the shoes in Zion looking glass.

But look, I turn man and start my little higgler business right here on the street. A poor man still, but my own man. You understand. And I save my one-one cocoa and I go to a balm woman to wash off my heart. St. Thomas she come from. She put me in a basin and wash me down with all kinda country leaf and powder. She burn two red candle. And after she done, she say, I going to give you deliverance.

The balm woman sleep with me and whisper compellance in my ears—she was nice that way—but she take all my money, and afterwards I still dream-see the Chinie-man at night, his eyes on me. And no matter what shoes I buy, them never the same as the one the mad-angel did shine. For God be my judge, I go Zion gate and see myself in those shoes. I wish I could get two vision-shoes like that—

NORVAL

Bob's Faadah Has His Say

As I walked away from Nesta, I didn't know what to do with my arms, so I put my hands in my pockets and tried to hold my head straight. A little girl across the street pointed and said, "Look the white man a cry," and I wiped my face with my cuff. Call me lily-liver if you want. That night, I took an exercise book and wrote on the pages fast, back and front, back and front:

Iamacowardwhitecowardwhitemancowardjamaicawhiteman—

"Is you mi faadah?" Nesta's little voice picked at me like a mosquito. And he looked like me too—my name written all over his face. The long bridge of his nose, the slanted forehead—me in dark skin. But the lips, the star-apple stained lips, those were Cedella's. I fancied her to madness. She was beautiful in that over-ripe, black country girl sort of way. And I was the white man in the district; the white man on a horse. She was young, but nobody, except the father, cross-questioned me. And even he turned his face the other way after a while. But I never meant for it to go so far. For in the end, what can a man like me, a white man, a soldier with bloody England in his veins, do with a little black country gal like that? Then came the child. The marriage to make things respectable. By the time the rest of the Marleys found out, they were outraged. Could I bring the boy to visit, I dared ask. The room was so quiet, you could slice the silence and serve it on a plate. Oh the look on mother's face! This woman who liked to remark that her Steinway was the only black to ever step-foot in the family. And there in the silence the thought came: nobody has ever played her old piano. It had come on a steamer from London, the inside of the stool filled with barbiturates and packaged with a relative of a relative's used trousseau. In December 1883, it arrived in Kingston harbour, scratched and broken and out of tune, and after clearing it from the docks, nobody could afford to fix it. It had remained off-key for as long as I could remember.

Mother put her hand on the piano and eased herself up from the chair. Her feet were unsteady and the loose skin of her jowls shook. I took one look at her and knew I could not keep the boy. As she turned her back and walked into the bedroom, I began to cry. "Stop it, Norval! Just stop it!" she said. She would cut me off, disinherit me quick as a lightning bird, I knew that. There I was; in my sixties; my pockets empty; only a pound and five shillings in my wallet.

I got rid of the boy. What would Cedella care? Her son would do better out of the country-bush anyway.

MAMA

Mama Talks Back

Shut yu mouth! Is not me throw Nesta away, is him faadah throw him away! He take mi boy-chile, said he was going to send him to a good school in Kingston. The liard. How was I to know that he would just give Nesta away to strangers like that? Give him away, just like that to an old woman—Miss Grey. Miss Grey too old to even knot her own stocking much less make a decent cup of tea to offer mi pickney. But God bless her soul, she did her best by him. One whole year, I don't hear from Norval. The rat disappear. Is only by the grace of God, a woman see Nesta pon street and come a Nine Mile to tell me. But you know what? I don't hold nothing gainst Norval. Let bygones be bygones. My womb bless. What the builder rejected has become the chief corner stone. You see me here? I am a bless woman. Sometimes when I think about it, you know. Sometimes when I think about it, my heart just rejoice. Look at my children. Look at my grandchildren. Look at my great-grands. Look how my table spread pretty in the presence of mine enemies. Almighty! No, I don't hold nothing gainst Norval. Not a thing. It was so long ago, I can barely even remember what he look like. When I look at Bob is not Norval I see, you know. No, is His Majesty I see! His Majesty-self, Almighty Jah.

FROM THE HUMMING OF LIONS IN THE GARDEN OF JAH

Track 20.0: The Seat of the Most High

For years, H.I.M. had tossed at night, fearful of backbiters and unable to sleep, but now that Riva Man had come, it was the duty of the Jamaican to sweep and protect the chamber. Each morning, Riva Man swept the twelve corners of the Most High's suite, cleansing it of the previous night's bad dreams, of the plots of enemies, and the malcontent of warring ancestors. He swept, Jah live, Jah live, until the chamber was peaceful ground.

Night, the Most High entered his apartment and quickly forgot his concerns—the crocodile teeth in the Minister of Culture's mouth, the odd scent of absinthe in the afternoon tea. He slept curled on his side, facing east, soothed by the cleansed, well-swept room.

Each afternoon, Riva Man bound new thatch, for the old broom carried the weight of the previous day's worries and could not be used again. The thatch was gathered carefully from palms he tended himself. Only the stick of the broom remained constant, made from a sycamore tree, and engraved with hibiscus buds and blossoms of oleander—same like Aaron's rod in the Book of Numbers.

Riva Man served the King of Kings seven years and forty-four days. And in all of those years, not one hair on the Most High was singed. For Riva Man swept in silence; and in Jamaica, Rastafari chanted down Babylon;

and across the island the smoke of holy herb rose up,
wondering at the inner chamber of Jubilee Palace.

Jah-live.

HERE-SO; HALF WAY TREE

Pharmacy

There is a woman standing in front of York Pharmacy. She has her back turned and is looking at a sign in the window, one loc hanging loose from beneath a yellow head-wrap. Something about the loc reaching towards ground, thirsty for water, makes Bob cross the street. He stands there behind the woman for just a moment before she catches his reflection in the glass, her eyes meeting his—watching him watch her through the window.

"*Dawta of Zion.*" His voice is like nutmeg on an old grater and Leenah *hears* it. She puts her hand to her mouth in disbelief, watching his lips as he sings the song written for her. At the end of it, she stands silent, still watching him in the glass.

"You want to know how to run Rastaman duppy?"

"Fry up pork in hot oil and add plenty salt," she says.

A girl absorbed in a book goes into the pharmacy, a blast of cool air coming from the open door.

"Is you the conqueror."

"But of course."

"You never did tell me how you turn deaf," Bob says.

His words are earnest, and Leenah answers as if she had been waiting at the shop window for his question for years:

"I heard a wickedness and paid the price. I was looking for jimbilin behind a zinc fence when I heard two men talking and plotting wickedness against Rasta. They were going to burn down a record studio; too much dutty Rasta in it. And they were going to kill people too. Your song was on the radio. I tried to keep quiet but one of them heard me cough and quick jumped on me and held me down as the other took something like a bicycle spoke and rammed it down one of my ears and then the next. For a moment there was no pain. I heard a pop and it was as if my head cleared—everything beautiful and quiet like the bottom of an underground cave—and then he pulled the spoke from my ear and there was a rush of air like a mad torrent surging through me. I opened my mouth to scream, only I couldn't hear myself. It was like in a dream—opening your mouth, but no sound coming out. He was yelling something, his mouth moving, Shut up shut up; I couldn't hear him but I knew what he was saying, Shut up shut up; and all at once there was Mama's voice, Leenah! I *heard* her voice as if from far away and my scream became a roar; I knew I was roaring because I felt it in my body. The way lions know they are roaring in their dreams. The roar filled me up, entered my brain and my eyes; I bit into the man's jaw, tasting his blood in my mouth. The other man had to pull him away and they both took off, running like mongoose lightning."

When she is done speaking, she still does not turn around for she has the distinct feeling that if she looks at him directly, Jah light on his face will be unbearable. Leenah stands, trembling in front of the window-glass. And Bob, as if understanding, touches her lightly on the shoulder.

"Is alright," he says. "I&I come back; have no fear."

"Unfinish business."

"Spirit tings. Or maybe me just come back—to see Zion dawta."

"Bless."

He kisses her neck and she feels the hum of it and shivers. He breathes in her scent.

"The angel want your ras berry. It written in the book."

She turns around then, taking in the breadth of him. He takes the book from his satchel.

"All I&I have is this."

And she remembers. It is the book the angel carried the night he came to the window.

"And this."

And he holds up the wooden staff and takes out the shoe brush and polish and the transistor radio.

"And one more thing."

And he shows her the ring wrapped in toilet paper.

Anjahla comes out of the pharmacy. She has Leenah's eyes and lips and fierce cheekbones. "Mama?"

She goes quickly to her mother's side, pulls her away from the tall man with the chime earrings.

"Meet me at the clock in five years," Bob calls.

FROM BLOODFIAH, RECORD OF DREAMSLOST

Track 9.0. 1978: In the Middle of the Middle of the Night

This shu-shu has never been told. One night while Bob slept, Negus touched the prophet's forehead with a tamarind switch. It was late and Bob was sprawled on his bed, dreaming of galloping on a horse across an African savannah. The horse had stripes of black musical score against its white hide—the riddim bass and bloodfiah in Bob's ears. Its chorus repeated over and over and Bob knew that as soon as he awoke, he would reach for his guitar and write the words.

When the horse paused to drink from a red stream, Negus slipped the Judah ring off the prophet's finger. Bob turned in his sleep and pulled his hand away, but did not wake up. As the horse broke into a trot, Negus replaced the ring with an imitation, then tucked the original under his tongue. It was the next night that he went to see the ripe mango woman, Leenah, and climbed in through her window.

The truth is, Negus intended to give back the ring, but fell down-down into pestilence and tribulation before it could be returned to Bob's middle finger. That falling afternoon when he awoke on Hellshire beach, he fished it from under his tongue, dropped it in his pocket and no one ever knew a thing.

Later, after Bob's cancer-foot passing, there was big banga: This one wanted the ring sealed in the mausoleum and that one wanted it returned to Ethiopia. This one wanted it sold for thirty pieces of silver and that one wanted it returned to the right hand of Jah. This one wanted it behind glass in a museum showcase and that one wanted it worn on their babyfinger. Only Fall-down knew that the fight over the rightful place for the ring was fought over an imitation. The half, Almighty Jah, has never yet been told.

LEENAH

Rastaman Vibration

I heard Bob; I heard him. Right here-so, in front of York Pharmacy. The words were Bob's I'm sure. So was the scent of herb and coconut oil, the kerosene lamplight in the eyes. But the lips were those of the angelman in the dream. The height and the breadth of him. And the earrings, the little brass Africas—I remember them against my skin the night he drank from my navel. Today at the window, a roar ignited my tailbone for the second time. I looked at the reflection behind me, and knew right away it was Bob and all my words sped out of my mouth for there was a feeling that I needed to make haste like when a star falls and you speak quick—

The last time I saw one drop was the night they buried Bob. The sky over Jamaica does not give up stars easily. Bob would have said: "Jah stars no fall; them rise." Maybe it all depends on what window in the cosmos you are looking from. When I&I saw that star rise, I made a wish quick-quick that I would hear Anjahla's voice.

And then, Anjahla came out of the pharmacy. I saw her lips move. She pulled me away to the car; she always thinks she needs to protect me. Meanwhile, I heard Bob clear-clear like small stones raining in a field of silence. He called after us, *Meet me at the clock*—

So I&I will wait; five years. Babylon goes on. I never did finish at UWI—the university not ready for deafspeak. But I make brooms, art brooms—ornate and handcarved—long necks that balance sistah-queen heads on top; I thatch them up nice, like Riva Man showed me. No money in the brooms but I do social work, bringing arts and culture to deaf-Kingston. Anjahla comes with me sometimes; she is in high school. She likes butterflies and moths, and writes stories about frogs that fly. My patient at Mt. Olive Nursing Home is Mrs. M.; she is the only deaf there; and the nurses don't know what to do with her. She likes the picture I show of Michelangelo's finger touching the fingertip of God. Then I show one I did—me reaching for the fingertip of Jah. She smiles, covering her mouth and peering at the ring on his His Majesty's finger. "I like it," she signs. Mrs. M. has bright eyes but is no bigger than a rat-bat. Michelangelo would have loved to paint her. She likes to wear a black nightgown and stick red hibiscus in her hair. She says it is the gown she wore on her wedding night. I picture Mrs. M. beautiful that night, her skin smooth and her princess-neck gown showing cleavage. In 1927, she must have been a knockout in black satin. The nurses call her crazy. She arrived one Boxing Day with some clothes in a suitcase, a cosmetic bag and a Bible. Her son hardly turned his back before a nurse raked through her things and snatched the Jean Nate talcum powder from the bag. It turned out that there was salt in the tin. Another nurse found a dead roach in a bottle of face cream. Mrs. M. sat on a chair by the bed and pretended to doze. I have liked her ever since.

One afternoon she reaches for my hand and does not let go. She unfurls my fingers and opens my palm, careful as a present. She is excited about something, her mouth a little beak opening and closing. "Look. There it is." She points to a line right under my forefinger, a crescent carved into the skin. A nurse who has been watching from her corner-eye on the other side of the room, comes over to look. Mrs. M. kisses my palm like treasure. Her lips are brittle, little bits of dry skin scratching my hand-middle. "That line. See—right there—the Ring of Solomon."

So that was why Riva Man smiled when he saw my hand. I waited twenty years to find out. Some people have a clear line for fame, a long line for life, a curved little finger. They say that those who have the ring of Solomon have the gift of second sight. Second sight? Bullshit. A deaf woman good at reading lips and making signs, that's all. I don't see people's minds. If I could, I would not have needed to listen behind the zinc fence; I would have already seen Papa's head roasted on the ground; I would not have called Verle, Elizabitch; and I would know where to find Mama's loc.

All this went through my mind as I looked at the crescent under my finger. Curved like a small wry smile. It took me a while to realize that I *do* see what others don't. I saw the six-finger woman at Mama's bedside; too, I recognized and *heard* Bob in the pharmacy window and maybe in a funny kinda way, I foresaw Verle's death in the middle of the street, and if I am willing to think back through macca and coral vine, there are other things too. Like the angel. But why did Bob appear in the angel's skin? I am afraid of I-self.

Barbary lions are in the news. They were thought to be extinct, but then someone found some standing at the brink of death in a zoo in Addis Ababa. Seeing Bob in Half Way Tree fifteen years after his passing was like finding those Barbary lions. Can a roar return from extinction?

FROM THE HUMMING OF LIONS IN THE GARDEN OF JAH

Track 13.0: Barbary

They say the Barbaries were waiting at the palace gate when the Queen of Sheba returned from the land of Israel. More ancient than the very dirt on King Solomon's shoes, they roamed Northern Africa—the females with keen, intelligent faces and a watch-yu-self roar; the males with dark manes that extended to the groin. They were the lions the Romans fed the Christians to. And the lions that guarded the Queen of Sheba's newborn son.

Everyone thought the last Barbary roared in 1922, shot by a hunter, until, sixty years later, eleven were discovered in an Addis Ababa zoo—descendents of the lions that once roared in Selassie's palace garden. They had been put in the zoo to humble the Most High, but those lions kept on roaring. They had roared when Mengistu's men arrested H.I.M. at the Jubilee Palace, taking him away in the blue VW. They roared when they slaughtered H.I.M.'s household and ransacked his papers, threw his small body in Ethiopia's sewage. Descendents of a dynasty of Barbary, which had defended the very gates to the ark of Jah-Jah covenant, they would not stop now. Rasta live.

When they lived as queens and kings among fig trees and bougainvillea in the garden, H.I.M. fed them bits of meat from a gold-plated dish. He always had a way with animals, especially lions. They understood him as kin-folk. "There, there," he would say, stroking their chin and tossing a bit of meat from the plate with his seal, "there, there."

FROM THE ANGEL'S LEDGER BOOK

[Page 1,493: Tambourines]

September, 1910—Young Tafari's sheets smell of peppermint. Tonight he dreams of a girl who smothers him with a pillow, then lets him out for menthol just before he asphyxiates. She throws back her head and laughs and does it again. He likes this dream and does not wish to leave.

Twelve angel's trumpet blossoms fall at 2:47 a.m. in the east garden.

The boy and his father, Makonnen, pose for a picture. Neither of them smile. "People will shoot arrows through the very gaps in your teeth, if you let them," says Makonnen. Tafari remembers this all his life.

The moon over Addis Ababa has a yellow haze around it. Hyenas skulk the outskirts of the city. Tafari turns in his sleep and wishes for the girl to return.

April 6, 1962—An earthquake shook Addis Ababa today. The emperor was sitting at his desk when the brass lion used as a paperweight fell on its side. An old letter from the empress was on top. Afterwards, he reported a headache and had to lie down.

August, 2000—A man, Sebaut Gebre Yesus, has opened a museum in Addis Ababa. He has included the emperor's old iron bed and other personal effects collected over the years.

HERE-SO; HALF WAY TREE

Star

Bob draws another star on the ground with a piece of stone. The points of the star uprise like a lion's mane. He circles a tail around the top, pondering Jah-time. There is something else he understands now. At first, he counted them in fives, but the number of years between mornings could well be arbitrary. He gazes down the road at the clock tower. It is now a quarter to three. A breeze lifts up a girl's dress. Jah wind does not blow by appointment. If Leenah comes in five years, she will probably miss him. He tosses the stone and sits on the curb; listens to the car stereos and the new-time music with its too much electric and double treble. *More bass, people, more bass. Bass is the root.*

Management does not want him standing outside the pharmacy, so he walks down a little way, pacing pharmacy, gas station, and post office, watching people lick their stamps and drop letters in the box. Something is about to happen in Half Way Tree. He feels it.

A thought comes to him that he could post a letter to Rita, but he quickly lets it go. Where she is now anyway? Two schoolboys throw an empty box drink at him.

"Bet you don't come little closer," Bob calls.

One of them edges nearer, a big grin on his face, and Bob takes out the ring from the toilet paper.

"This ring for your lunch money," he says.

The boy looks at the ring and is about to reach for it when the other one pulls him back.

"Look the mad man wrap the ring in the same paper him use wipe him batty. And is a play-play ring; it don't even worth nothing." They both run off.

Half Way Tree smells of dog pee-pee and rotten june plum. The traffic light changes, red green and gold over and over.

"This ring for a money," he says. "This ring for a cool drink."

The post office closes and he decides to forward in the other direction, reason with the Rasta breddren. But everything change-up and the Aquarius Record Shop is not there anymore; there is a shop selling shoes in its place. He walks toward the place Delroy sells bottle water. The youth called him faadah and he denied it. He wished now he had kept his mouth shut, the pain-o-heart on Delroy's face was only a flicker, but it was real. You can't suck words back.

Delroy has not yet packed up for the day; he looks tired. "Ras?"

"Me sorry me had was to leave for them years," Bob says. "A father should not pick up and go just like that."

There is a brief silence between the two; like a scratchy pause between vinyl songs.

"No worry. You're a fall-down angel. Remember?"

Bob smiles and looks down at his palms. Such linelessness makes him feel like nobody—and everybody.

"So you think the ring worth anything?" He takes it out of his pocket again.

"You still have it? Is what them call a reproduction, I tell you. Is not a bad one though—you might get something for it. But the real one now—that one priceless. Bob bury with it. But don't you know more about them things than me?"

The lights are still red; pedestrians cross.

"Me no remember no ring in the coffin. I did have mi guitar and someone did put an icey-mint in mi mouth, still wrap in the paper; the wig on mi head like one dread barrister to—" And then he catches himself—it's useless to talk about himself as Bob. Delroy hands him back the ring. "But I-man no need material things. Just a box drink and two patty me looking."

DUB-SIDE CHANTING

Track 19.0 Dis Appointment

Already three days have passed and Bob is not back yet. Fall-down kicks at a stone. He is ready to return to Half Way Tree. He has left his staff there and his canvas bag with his ledger of hap-pen-tings. He misses the dust and the grime of Kingston. The smell of urine and rotting fruit behind the bus stop, the john crows overhead searching for dead prey. He misses the traffic and the heat so thick he can swallow it like mucus. He misses Delroy with his play-play guitar and dutty mouth. The women across the street with their cut-eye and slow walk. He misses macca and orange love bush and pink coral vine. And what wouldn't he give for two patty and a box drink?

But more than all this, he wants Leenah. To climb on her windowsill, the way he did in her dream. This time, she will wake up; no true? If you fall, you should at least enjoy the thing you have fallen for.

But this. This place is like getting caught stealing a mango, and not able to eat it. Leenah is somewhere in Kingston, he is sure. And sooner or later, all roads lead to Half Way Tree. He needs to get back there. This place with its ganja fog and trees breathing in and out makes him feverish. And where is Bob?

STUDIO Z
HECTOR

Track 18.5: What the Pulse Knows

There in his little house, Hector has moved his sewing machine out to the veranda. Cerulean blue suits bulge through the windows now. He waves to no one in particular and takes a sip of the coconut water in his cup, a huge smile on his face. The little tags on his suits read, "Made in Zion."

FROM THE ANGEL'S LEDGER BOOK

[Cathedral of Gongs]

February 6, 1978—The ring Bob wears is the same one that was worn by the Emperor. It was the Emperor's favourite, given to him by his father, Makonnen.

June 26, 1934—The Emperor has made 77 exact copies of the ring to protect from thieves and confuse the plots of the unrighteous. The original is kept in Axum.

July 23, 1906—It is Tafari's fourteenth birthday. His father gives him a scroll of twenty-one poems, Les Vingt et Un. The poems are written in black ink in the poet, Rimbaud's, own hand. The youth copies the words to improve his French. He makes twenty-one copies of the twenty-one poems. The original he tucks into the beams of the ceiling where he keeps a milk tooth and a letter he wrote to a girl, but did not dare deliver.

Tafari likes the last poem of Les Vingt et Un best. It is reckless with desire, written for Rimbaud's Ethiopian mistress. Tafari commits the words to memory and recites them late night as he fondles himself beneath the covers.

The mistress's name is Mariam. The angel, Negus, knows her well. He counts thirteen moles on her skin—three on her belly, five on her thighs, four across her shoulders and one on the back of her heel.

April 2, 1895—The angel is there when Rimbaud interprets the constellation of Mariam's skin. After the revelation of her heel, Rimbaud forgets why he ever needed to be a poet. And in the forgetting, becomes a truer poet.

Rimbaud gives Les Vingt et Un to his friend, Ras Makonnen, like giving away old clothes.

Recitation Day, 1906—In Tafari's dream, Rimbaud's mistress is a young girl of seventeen. He stands before her and recites the poem with such passion it is as if he wrote it himself. Mariam sits with her face in her hand, and listens. "Do not forget this dream," she says. "Mark it with your eyelid. From now on, the only copy of Les Vingt et Un exists here, in sleep." She kisses him on his mouth, takes the poems and puts them beneath her shawl.

When Tafari awakes he remembers the dream but can no longer recite the poem. He searches the beams, but the poems are not there; neither is the letter to the nobleman's daughter; only the tooth remains.

It has been raining all day in Harar. Tafari is too embarrassed to inquire of the letter, and dares not unleash his father's anger at his carelessness with Les Vingt et Un.

Each night the boy searches the archives of his sleep.

February 6, 1978—It is said that bits of gold from King Solomon's ring exist in the Emperor's Judah Lion.

If this is so, then the Emperor's ring is the great-great-great-great-great-great-great-great-great-grandchild of King Solomon's.

But not even the angel knows if this is true. Can truth be both created and destroyed?

HERE-SO; HALF WAY TREE

Back in Town

Middle of the night and Bob awakes in the clock tower to a foot tapping. He gets up and lights a candle—only a spider works in the corner. She is black and long-legged and ropes revolution. But it is not her foot he hears. A man leans against the locked door. He is short and stout; his face in shadow, watching the spider.

"My wife—the second one—she was an industrious woman, just like that spider." The voice is low, with no bottom. "Her name was Amy. I married two times, two women both with the same name. Amy and Amy. My, my."

The candle catches the lines of the man's face; the big cheeks, the moustache, the neck thick in the tight collar.

"My father was a mason and knew how to build a good house," he says. "But that spider, she builds with eaves and buttresses like a cathedral."

His jacket is buttoned neat over a fat tummy.

"What if she could build us a ship like that, back to Africa?"

The spider shivers, and keeps on going.

"You talk like a book what me read already. Like me know you." Bob holds the candle closer to the man's face.

"My name is Marcus," the man says. "Garvey. I wish I had not died in England, but see me here, back where I began. This time, we must call on the past to move us forward, rally the ancestors if we need to."

JAHJAH JAHJAH JAHJAH ᴊᴀʜᴊᴀʜ. Two aluminum cans knock up in the breeze. The prayers of a woman crossing the street: *My daughter in the mouth of the dragon, America. What kinda Babylon. Falling-falling; I see it in a dream.* Children laugh at two dogs in heat in the park across the street. Gun shot in the distance. A woman spray paints NOIZ on concrete. A baby in a trashcan sneezes.

"The people have summoned us back." Marcus takes off his jacket. Underneath he wears a velvet vest and white shirt. He takes off the vest and rolls up the sleeves of the shirt. "They must have called us with every last fibre of their being. Sometimes rockbottom will do that to a people."

"Music is how me stir up the people. But my voice scratch now, and no one know I&I name."

"Brother, let us do as the spirit moves. I too am limited in my ways. Each time I leave the clock tower, I become as a pea dove. Who would believe it? Marcus Garvey, a pea dove."

"Jah call the humble of the earth to confound the mighty. Even a bird shall lead them."

"Yesterday I preached fire and brimstone from a government rooftop, blazed a cry of liberation with my beak. Yes, I flew into the middle of high-noon court session and upset the corrupt from their seats. A pea dove can peck out the eyes of the unrighteous; guide the weary home."

"But can it build a ship to take the people to Africa?"

"This is what I know now. The people need a different fleet."

FROM THE ANGEL'S LEDGER BOOK

[Priest's Bells]

February 15, 1962—Queen Menen has passed. Her pale hands are fragile as moth wings.

His wife gone, at night the Conquering Lion is alone in bed; the Angel sends the woman, Mariam, to his dream. It has been 56 years since they last met, but in dreams time makes no haste. She takes the poem from under her shawl; the paper perfumed with ylang ylang. The Emperor reads it and becomes as a young boy. Mariam smiles and rises from the rattan chair.

In the morning the Emperor remembers only one word: rouge.

And rouge is everywhere—roadside hibiscus, the seeds of a pomegranate, a piece of velvet—such obsessions are a distraction. The Emperor is annoyed at himself for being so taken by the poem of a ferenji. What is the lesson to be learned here?

October, 1935—Italian troops loot Ethiopia. Mussolini takes the obelisk from Axum; many treasures are stolen. This Mussolini means to find the Ark of the Covenant. The pope wants it.

There are 100 exact copies of the Ark of the Covenant. The original is behind a red curtain. Somewhere.

There are 33 red curtains of the same sort.

October 4, 1963—The Emperor speaks to the United Nations. "We Africans will fight, if necessary, and we know that we shall win, as we are confident in the victory of good over evil." Africa will not be shaken.

Bass Day, 1976—Bob Marley turns the Emperor's speech into a song. The women who love him see the way he closes his eyes when he sings it. The angel watches the women watch Bob.

When he sings, Bob feels everything. And the angel sees everything.

HERE-SO; HALF WAY TREE

From the Mouth of a Pea Dove

"Give thanks and praise for the great-man who school I&I in the history of I&I people."

There is a woosh of wind outside. Something crashes against the door. A string of wailing and car horns wraps around the clock. The voices fast forward to an old woman: *Weevils take up the shop flour.* And then there is a mighty singing, a seven-layered chorus of many people. The voices shake the foundations, and at the tail end of it, a small child hums. Bob pushes against the door to open it, but the chorus begins again and his arms are not strong enough against the breath of so many. He must wait until the years pass over.

"Emancipate yourself from mental slavery," Garvey says to no one in particular.

"Your words, Uncle."

"When we do this, Africa will be united."

The air outside is filled with reverb. AFRICA-RICA RICA-RICA.

"Me have a bone to pick with you still." Bob lights a spliff and passes it to Garvey. Garvey shakes his head, No thanks; no thanks. He looks Garvey in the eyes, prophet to prophet, his head is filled with lambsbread. "You prophesy of a black king and when he come, you call him coward."

"I did say that."

"Reason with me."

"The Italians invaded Ethiopia and the big-man fled to England, like a sissy. An emperor should hold fast with his people. All Africa was watching."

"But you find yourself in England too; and same time as His Majesty. Don't is England you dead?"

"I died before I could see the end from the beginning. Before I could witness victory in the lion's return. Death robs us that way." Garvey looks up at the rafters; the spider is busy. "He was positioned to unite all of Africa, that man. I was angry with him. And I admit, just between the two of us, there had been times when a part of me envied him even. Oh to be emperor of all Africa."

Yes-I, flies a voice outside.

"Yes-I," says Bob.

"But let us not bicker. The people have not called us back to wallow in smallness; they have called us because of our greatness. Let us hold together and let us not disappoint."

"Me always only have one goal, to see everybody live-up, together. Is for that me sing."

"Go out and sing then; sing the message with your scratched voice. Sing from the rooftops, sing from the gullies, just sing. The people have called you back with their music and tears. Do you know what it takes to call a spirit home?"

SPIRITHOME-SPIRITHOME-SPIRITHOME goes the dub reverb outside.

Garvey's eyes are red, and moist.

"Our people are magicians," he says.

The ancestor roots of the old cotton tree shift underground, reaching for water, for the roots of such a tree do not die easily. They stretch downward and across, under the street, all the way to Mandela Park. Lizards feel the roots move and so do soldier ants and mice. There is a small twelve-plait girl who stands across the street, facing the clock; she feels it too.

All night Bob and Marcus Mosiah Garvey chant Nyahbinghi.

"Tonight, I am a Rastaman," Garvey says, and they chant for the old women crossing the street/for the schoolchildren with no lunch money/for the pregnant dawta holding her belly/the youth leaning gainst the clock tower/for the man on his way home from burying his children/the mangy dog in the road/the woman with a gun in her brassiere/the muddy feet in the betting shop/the son with a bees in his lung/and the girl in York Pharmacy, looking

176

bleach-cream for mahogany/the woman on the bus with cocaine in her vagina/the child with no daddy/the grandmother at the stop-light with the spoiled milk/the baby blown from his mother's arms by hurricane/by hurricane/by hurricane/for murdered trees and maimed birds/for fish in the sea, and the firmament under the sea/and for fiah-fiah catching the heart of the firmament/for Xaymaca, this land of wood and sweet riva-wata.

They chant.

HERE-SO; HALF WAY TREE

Next Day: Year of Rain and Wind [200?]

Next morning there is a black and green bird with a red beak in the lignum vitae tree across from the square. When Bob slips out the door, it takes off and marks a circle in the sky. He follows the bird all the way to Maxfield Ave.; it criss-crosses gulley and lane; love-bush and barbed wire. He is glad his legs are long and quick.

At Three Miles, the bird perches on the back of a red pick-up truck; Bob hops a ride too. The driver—an old man—hums redemption hymns and drops Bob in front of a racehorse betting shop. The bird squawks up above and Bob steps up his stride. He passes a corner which he recognizes as a place he used to sit and play guitar. People stopped, and put down their bags, and listened there.

And little ways down—the gate where he would stand and sweet-talk Rita; she was young then, and had eyes like his mother's. There was kindness on her face, and sufferation too, and strength. For a moment now, he misses her; she was the one who knew him the most. She hummed back-up; and she watched his back and washed it too. He pauses at the gate, remembrance flooding down—the children, the tours, the bad feelings, the fighting. Forward to that day when he pressed his palms against her windshield, and she screamed and did not know him. Maybe he should have recite their palangpang in the street, shout it out to rhaatid. Things only him and she woulda know. She would have recognize him then, no-true? But really, you want to know Bob vice?

The bird squawks again, leading Bob deeper into concrete and zinc, to places unfamiliar. They pass a yard where a group of children poke a dead dog with a stick. Down a lane of zinc, a woman throws dirty dishwater over a fence, a lizard in the water. Road block. A youth with a rifle stands in the middle of the road. Across the street, a goat roped to a tree, bleats with no sound. At the opposite corner a girl sits on a stool reading a book. Bob stops and she looks up, as if expecting him. Duppy, she says; and the iris in her left eye strays to one side. Bob reaches for the book; the words inside hum, but the girl pulls it back; her eyes say, *Not now.*

"I want to know mi true name," he says. "You find I&I name yet? It written down in the book? The girl spits out her gum, keeps on reading and does not look up.

There is a breeze coming up from the south. The bird waits on an electric wire, preening the green of its belly. It takes off and Bob has to run to keep up as the youth with the rifle takes a gangster pose, spreads his legs and shoots—the bullet ricochets off the radio in Bob's satchel, sound busting out big-so. The reverb sends people to their windows, some in the street. Wha dis? They stand and watch the madman run.

No one notices the bird in the whirlwind; they think the madman running from gunshot. Someone's salt-fish and onion burns in hot oil. The Africas at Bob's ears jingle ting&ting; the red scarf on his head is wet around the edges. He longs for a drink of water, the sort that has its source in deepness. He runs without seeing, sweat in his eyes, guided only by the bird call.

LEENAH

Bone

Five years to the day, I wait for Bob in front of the clock, but do not see him. I stand with my back against the door, watching the street. No Bob. I go the next day too, but then after that I feel like a fool. Still, I know I saw what I saw. It was Bob in the mad man's skin. I will return in five more years.

Tonight, the lions in my dream are old; their manes are grey like Rasta elders and their roar holds the history and herstory of everything; I wallow in the wild of it, criss-crossing salt and sugar islands, riding seas, walking the perimeter of Africa. When we get to the Red Sea, I traverse easily for I recognize it as woman's blood. We cross Eritrea and the border to Ethiopia, spanning centuries. I roar with the lions and we awake every living creature in livity and oneness, all of them in all of me, right here-so. This is how I learn the true meaning of I&I. And then there is laughter and I turn to see a young girl skipping in a field of blue flowers. One day your bones will be discovered, she says. She speaks a strange language, which I find I understand. It is filled with innuendo and physical sensations; the word for *bone* so strong that the sound of it reverbs through the dream to my shin and into my foot-bottom. I wake up laughing, the syllable of bone echoing way-way out to the future.

Anjahla is at the door in her pyjamas; come to see what's so funny.

"What I sound like when I laugh?" I ask.

"You sound like an old hige at the beginning of time," she says.

"Time don't have no beginning and don't put any years on me," I say.

180

Anjahla rolls her eyes. "Go back to sleep, Mama," she says.

I sink in the pillow of blue flowers and wait for another dream. I want to hear Anjahla. I want to hear her say, Mama.

ANJAHLA

When I Call Your Name

Mama. Mama, can you hear me? At what speed does love travel underwater?

They say there is a laughter only rivamumma can hear.

They say if you play a record backwards, there are words there. And there are secrets in the scratchy silences between songs.

There is a riddim that loops from here-so, all the way across centuries. Ole-time people heard it layered under night rain.

If a sound is an echo, is it still real? Copies of copies of sound.

And if you find my voice in a fissure in your sleep, will it be less real?

Remember the babymothers who were forced to jump off the ships? Sometimes I hear their children calling, *Mama.*

Here's what I know: When I call your name, my voice is their echo—

RASTAMAN

Thirst

I-man run and run—follow the bird. I neva know Kingston so big—is like town a stretch, no have no end, till me get to some part me neva even know exist, so thick with zinc and barbwire trap. Me cross a place of bottle-glass and ole mash-up Austin Cambridge car; the car-them full with newspaper and Styrofoam cup and kerosene tin, and john-crow flying all around.

And then me see *one* coconut tree, stand up tall-tall, all by itself in the rubble. And the tree pretty so-till and it have *one* wata coconut, and the bird perch on it. Thirst parch me and the coconut wata calling me and I feel to climb this tree, tall as it is, for I&I is a country-man and me and plenty tree hold council together. Me put mi club-foot at the base of the trunk and that's when I&I see a little footpath behind. The wata in the coconut calling, but something tell me, *Step out on the path.* When my foot touch the ground, I&I feel it—a riddim of dread and chordstuck and tenement cry; it catch me up in a riff that play over and over, and nah let me turn back.

Then the bass line drop, and I&I know is this path I must trod—

DUB-SIDE CHANTING

Track 33.0: If the Foot Fit

Fall-down stands at the base of the nutmeg tree, searching for Bob's tracks in the dust. He finds one and puts his foot inside of it, hoping for the way back to Half Way Tree. He longs to find Leenah. To watch her undress through her Rasta curtain window. How many times did he do that when she was not looking? And to see once again the Africa birthmark on her thigh, a perfect fit for his earring to rest. He puts his foot in the next track and holds himself steady on Bob's short feet, looking for the other.

LEENAH

Can a Zebra Change Its Stripes?

I asked Bob about Rita once. "You still love her?"

He gave me the expected Bob answer, "I-man love every woman."

"That's a dodge answer," I said. "Answer me properly this time. I'm asking if you still love Rita. Don't you did marry her?"

"Marriage is a trap that don't serve we; is a Babylon trap. Who make that law? Tell me who make that law?"

"Do you love her?"

"Love no partial. Is only one-love me have. Same love me feel for that doctor bird, same love me feel for every woman."

"Don't use oneness as no bullshit cover. It too precious for that. Is a different thing I asking. You know what I'm asking. Do you love Rita?"

"Is the university a spoil you."

"Don't you did marry her? I hear you on the radio-show the other night denying it thrice, but don't you did marry her?"

I always pushed Bob like that. You had to push him to peel back the layers, or else you would only get his one-love, or hope to glimpse him in passing in a song. It's true he interested me—his good looks, yes, and urban tough and country charm, but then there was his connection to spirit. And this is what truly bonded us. Of course, there was the whole dance to get me in bed, but I always knew, and I think he knew too, there was something else to our friendship.

And then he told me the story of how him and Rita met: the hard times in Trench Town and how they struggled together. He never did say he loved her, but I felt the vibration in his throat that told me there was a place in his heart for her. I respected that.

And there was the time, I asked him about his father. The whiteman on the horse.

"He hurt you, Bob?"

I saw something well up, but he would not let it fall.

We smoked herb in my room in Ms. Ivy house. We reasoned the halfness of being both white and black.

"But fully human," he said.

"And fully Jah."

"Fully woman, you."

"Yes, and fully Jah."

"What if Jah was a woman?" He surprised me with this one.

"She is," I said.

FROM THE ANGEL'S LEDGER BOOK

[Voice Archive]

September 12, 1974; Addis Ababa—Today the Dergue took H.I.M. into captivity. He surrendered as a lamb to the slaughter; did not say a word. The lions in the palace garden roared in his place.

November 24, 1974; Near Hadar—Even the ancestors cry out. They raise their bones on Ethiopia's behalf. Today they found the skull of one of them. They call her AL 288-1. They also call her Lucy. And they call her Dinkenesh—"You are amazing." The angel was there when she ran in a field of blue flowers.

And more ancestors will soon reveal themselves. Next time a three-year-old in Dikika. They'll call her Selam because she longs for peace. Hear how her bones cry when the men brush dust from her femur.

Hear this:

A woman at the bus stop has a gun in her brassiere/the light turns red and/a grandmother dreams of Zion-high/a schoolgirl sucks salt-water tears/pigeons pick mould from a piece of dry bread/green mangoes fall before they can ripe/sorry, no jobs/the baby's milk spoils in the hot sun/the clouds over Kingston heavy with cares-of-life tears/Public Works on strike/weevils in the flour/an eviction notice nailed to the door/rotten chicken-back in the market/sorry, no job/the children's coffins are made of pine/sorry, no/the goat tied to the ackee tree cannot bleat/sorry. The people are vexed with sufferation. Their tears smell like kerosene; soon Kingston will catch fiah.

Hear this:

If the stones do not cry out, then the dead will—Queen Nanny and Garvey and Sam Sharpe; or someone's fire-eye grandmoddah, or a flint-face aunt. The bass chord of the people's wail so trembles the ground, Bob hears it, the sound of pain-o-heart vibrating his bones at 30 Hz. The track is narrow, but not straight. It zig-zags down a slope and follows longside a wire fence, circles a tamarind tree. The bird gone, Bob walks with care on spirit feet. It is the evening of a hurricane warning, and except for a yellow dog, the streets are empty; the shops boarded up, concrete blocks securing the zinc roofs. The stillness is yellow, like the dog. A dusty yellow, a yellow that waits. The path joins a gully litter-litter with soda cans, old nails, bottle tops, rusty razors and sardine tins; the breeze makes percussion of the trash, a tinny chanting, soft at first, then growing louder. Someone has scratched red *war* on a wall. Bob traces the word with his finger, and rain begins to fall. And fall.

Rainwater fills and rinses every pore of him. He removes the scarf and it beats the roots of his hair; rushes down his spine and flushes the crack of his rump. He takes off his shoes and it beats between his toes. He cups his hand and drinks and drinks. All the while the dog watches from the shop piazza. Everything water. Bob lies down in the middle of the road and gives himself to the rain—

When the wind arrives, it hollers and dips, a wheel within a wheel. There is a metal drain at the curb and Bob grips the bars to brace himself. Water rushes; bits of zinc fly, a sheet of window glass, an enamel frying pan. He still holds fast to the drain as the wind lifts him in the air. See here: the pages of a book, a woman's fish knife, a bicycle wheel, the *ing* from a shop sign. Rain quickening—blood-fiah—the metal grate, a shield—

The wind whirls in the spirit then lands him—give thanks-and-praise—in a yard, dry and quiet and swept clean as holy ground.

*

The others have been waiting for his arrival in the eye. The bass riddim of the people has called them too. They lean against the zinc fence or sit on their haunches; some of them have bongo drums. There is a congregation of birds in an ackee tree and the smell of corn roasting on hot coals. A red flag blows from a bamboo pole. A woman steps forward.

They call me Queen Nanny, she says. Nanny of the Maroons. Is me could catch the white soldiers' bullets and spit them out. That is what the books say, but I used to do much more. I could grind a soldier's teeth and use the powder to light a good fire. I could spot one-a-them coming between the trees without turning around. I would feel it—the too-red of their jackets on my bare arm. One of them would piss behind a tree and I would hear it a mile off. If the books really said-all, the very ink would stink of blood. Let's leave it at that. But see me here; the people have called. I have heard their new-time music beating the ground, and the feet of the children, dancing, their hopefulness mixed with pain. Listen to me, there is an echo which travels along faultlines; it comes from their music. The strange music of the people. Sometimes the earth shudders and our bones move in their graves. How can we not arise?

189

Up, up ye mighty, someone sings.

An elder steps forward. His long grey locs touch his knees. He carries a staff carved with a Lion of Judah. My name is Leonard, he says. Leonard Howell. They call me the first Rasta, but that don't matter now. And they call me a thief, same like they call Garvey. Said I tricked the people with false tickets to Ethiopia. Thief or not, I had a vision. History needed me to keep the wheel turning.

Yes-I.

I come now to organize. To buoy the people up.

Up, up!

To higher groundation.

Praises.

Another woman steps forward. Her head is tied with a piece of flour bag. One furious plait twines against her face. Medon't have no name, she says. Everybody forget it and now not even me can remember it. It happen like that to plenty of we. We sew and plant and cook and sweep and wash and scrub and reap and stir and cry and pray and bend over and scream and break we back and then hold it straight again to send the children to school with piece of pencil so they can learn to write the book of we story and never forget it. I heard the babies crying from my grave—my grans and my gran's grans; and how could I not return?

Mercy.

A little girl wipes tears from her eyes. It was election time and gunshot fly into my face, straight up my nose, she says. Me step in front to save my brother. He was only three and Mama said to mine him while she go look one tin a mackerel. Me catch the shot just like Nanny, only it killed me. Me name Hortense, but them call me Tensie. From over this side, I hear my brother, big-man he is now, clicking a gun, and the sound of the click make my bones-them tremble. Don't! Don't! I call-out, but he can't hear me. I want to stop him. Help me stop him.

Stop the voilence! The people must stop it! Is long time we a warn them! A man steps forward. It is Garvey. He wears a green velvet vest under a black jacket. He has a hat of plumes. We must hold together now, he says. If the living have no hindsight, then we must be that hindsight. If the living have no foresight, then we must be that foresight. If the living have no wind, then we must be that wind. If the living have no fire, then we must be that fire.

Up, up. Let us be the terror and the tenderness, the storm and the lullaby. Let us whirl together as one mighty force—

Enough of the preaching to rah, a woman calls. She wears short-shorts and long white boots. Is Patsy me name. Even in the grave my feet keep dancehall. Me is a dancehall rebel woman. Is a rebel dance me a dance, for if you look the moves good, you see is Africa them come from, but the people don't know that. And me neva know it neither. Is Madda Nanny tell me. Is them kinda thing we need to tell the people. We don't need no more preaching.

Back to Africa. The people need Africa.

Garvey takes off his hat and holds it against his belly. Sister, you are right. This time we will need a ship of a different kind. The people must return to Africa on fleets of the mind. This is where Zion lives.

Yes-I. Yes-I.

We need a plan, Nanny says. Something great, same as we imagin-we-nation, yet simple as a goat's milk. That's how the Maroons defeated the enemy. Who woulda believe that we could defeat the British with a few roots and river stones and so-so weeds?

A woman dressed in white beats a drum between her knees. Three times three. Tears run down her face; her lips tremble. Three times three. Her hands call sound up/rising and/skin deliv/erance—

But how shall we start?

The drums stop. The woman falls to the ground, her body shaking. Someone sprinkles her with white rum. She lets out a sigh and everyone is quiet.

With the children, Bob says. He steps forward into the circle; still wet from the storm. My name is Robert Nesta Marley. I-man used to play music, but before that me was a boy had a pain in me heart. My heart so heavy it beat with a one-drop/one-drop. Is music and Rastafari save me, but everyone don't so lucky. The youth-them—me hear them bawl at night outside in the road. And when them eye-water dry-up, them beat them one another. Is them we must start with—

With one mighty force, calls Garvey.

The little youths shall lead us! One by one we must build an army.

Selah.

Somewhere a lizard begins to sing. The young girl, Hortense, rises up and Bob gives her the drum. Her small hands beat the skin, chanting down Babylon. The spirits sing Nyahbinghi, and Nanny dances in the circle. She grasps the hem of her skirt as her feet inch the ground, working the perimeter. There is a scent of white rum and a swirl of mango leaf and bird feather.

And this is what the drum speaks: Zion train coming/Zion train coming/People get ready/Zion train coming—

Zion is a place inside, calls Garvey.

And this is what the drum speaks: Set the children free/Set the children free/Set the children free.

Patsy zips up her boots and dances with Nanny in the circle. Who can't sing, clap; who can't clap, testify; who can't testify, dance! she calls. Her knees dip and part; dip and part. A draught travels her spine and rises to her head. It pushes at the space between her scalp and funeral wig. She closes eyes and whispers, Rah.

For this is what the drum speaks: Zion train coming/Zion train coming/Children get ready/Zion train coming—

And the woman with the furious plait begins to cry, for she sees her great grans far-far on the other side. They have her Guinea cheekbones and ashy skin. Zion is/a place inside! she calls, hoping they will hear. And her bare feet dance the words into the dust of the dirt yard. Zion/is, Zion is, her heels treading faster.

Zion is/Zion is/Zion is, go the drums. And spirit feet massage the ground—(for this is the real reason there are almost two hundred little earthquakes on the island per year, and why you should pay attention when the photo on the living-room wall shifts sideways, your feet unsteady in the hallway. For this is how the long-dead rock our fever babies or shake the youth from don't-care.)

But hear this:

Somewhere a schoolgirl sitting at a window/watches the rain/ feels the Nyahbinghi drum/beneath her feet/she scratches her foot-bottom and/turns the page of her note book/draws a map of a salt-and-sugar island/a boy sheltering in a chicken coop/feels it too/he plucks a make-believe guitar to the sound of rain and/ strums a new future/*the people will eat weevils if they have to*/*for what don't kill, will fatten*/this is the song the boy sings/and this is the map the girl draws/for the salt and the sugar must live together/don't salt stop you levitate?/but sugar can make rotten meat sweet?/*Take courage*/*take courage*/bleats the goat's heart/and a woman in a zinc house removes the gun from her brassiere/dries the tears from her eyes/nurses/a promised child.

And then/a great wind lifts Bob higher—

RASTAMAN

I-rical Quickening [in C major]

the rain it a fall it a fall. the wind it a blow it a blow. is a anti-clock wind this; wise-up yu-self/revolution deh-ya. quick-quick. quicken/

ing/wind blow a baby from the mother's arms. me catch it in me satchel and/hold it close. Kiss it before/wind steal it again—

for/this wind blow/Jah-Jah children like clothes/off the line. is long time me a warn you—hold them close/

the rain it a fall it a fall. the wind it a blow it a blow. is a anti-clock wind/this; wise-up yu-self/revolution deh-ya. quick-quick. en-quick/en

ing; wh/en hard time come, pickney frock fit yu—

The wind picks him up and blows him all the way back to Half Way Tree. He had thought that the spirit yard was the way—the passage of return to the right hand of His Majesty; the rest in peace of the home-sweet-home lamp; the lullaby of grated nutmeg sprinkled on milk. But the wind delivers him smack outside the clocktower door, and he is strangely glad of it—for there is work to do now and after tonight, there are only two days left.

It is quiet and dark in the clock. Bob lights a candle and sits down with his back against the wall. He reaches for the spliff, for each night it renews itself in his locs. He lights it like a sacrament. Breathes in and holds. Holds. Then exodus.

The smoke makes a white hibiscus above his head. He closes his eyes, remembers a video he made with children at a mock birthday party in London, maybe 1977. There were party hats and streamers and plenty cake. The children blindfolded him with ribbon and spun him round and around. They played cards together and juggled a yellow ball and he told them jokes. One boy with bright eyes pulled his locs and Bob let out a fart and everyone almost died. Is this love, is this love, is this love, is this love that I'm feeling? If he could have felt that high every moment of his life.

He opens his eyes and the hibiscus twines in front of him. Soon the clock tower is blooming with white flowers; hibiscus pollen falls on his face. One flower unfurls like a soft cloth and falls to the ground. Bob picks it up—a scarf—the smell like woodsmoke.

"Your locs hold the smell of mi one-daughter."

It is a woman's voice, but Bob cannot see her yet; the stems climb higher reaching for the rafters, and then he makes out a face amid the smokey flowers. She is tall and cedar, this dawtah. Jah-Jah empress dressed in white; her locs cover her bare shoulders. Cowries and red johncrow beads dangle at her ears. Something about her face is little bit familiar.

"I would know her smell anywhere," she says. "Like blood mix with frangipani blossom. Why you still hold her smell in your spirit hair?"

And when Bob does not respond, she takes the spliff from his hand and draws in smoke between her two ripe lips.

"She neva tell you mi name?" She hands back the spliff, and the smoke unfurls newborn birds from her mouth. She leans into the wall, smiles a smile of remembrance.

"I remember the day of the fire. She was so brave. I cut off one of my loc to give her, and she hold it in her fist like she coulda fight down Babylon right then and there." She reaches for the spliff again. This time the smoke rests in her hair, like wings in branches.

"I&I name Vaughn, Sistah Vaughn. Is Leenah me talking. And me have a grans now too, Anjahla." When she says, Anjahla, her lips shape each syllable as if very utterance of the name will set worlds in motion. And then she laughs, "Watch yu-self; is woman time now."

Bob is still watching the branches, wondering at the flock there. Leave it to Leenah to have a mother so beautiful.

"Leenah—me know her," is all he can say. "Me did want a baby with her." Vaughn sits on the floor in front of him; her skirt rises just above her bare feet. In the semi-dark, her toenails are bits of fall-down moon-ting. Bob reaches for the spliff.

"Is who Anjahla faadah?"

"Nobody know for sure. Not even she. But why you business with dat? Is true you love woman, but you was never one to let them distract you. And don't is only two days you have left?"

The birds in her hair have taken flight. Moths hatching from cocoons take their place.

"Tell me why you come."

"I smell mi one-chile in your hair."

"And is true that why you come check me?"

"I want you tell Leenah where mi loc bury. Is only you she can see, not me. I&I pinch her arm, and she think is mosquito; I shake the ice in her drink and she look at it strange, but don't know is me."

"Duppy inna second-hand skin. Is top ranking duppy dat." And

196

then he remembers—he was supposed to meet Leenah in front of the clock—

Vaughn takes the white scarf in her hands and wraps it around her head. With her locs pulled away, Bob notices her cheekbones, like Leenah's.

"The loc bury under the little cocoa tree in Leenah heart. Is she same-one take it and drop it there and then wind and rain and cares-of-life cover it."

The pods and tendrils rise higher. One end of Vaughn's scarf catches up in the unfurling.

"And me have a word for the children too," she says. "Tell them, Mt. Zion is a holy place."

The smoke makes a lid of higherstanding above them; they are quiet in the dark. Vaughn falls asleep on the floor and sleeps the sleep within sleep that only the dead can know. For at times, there is a peace this way. Bob watches her closed eye-lids and wonders is where the latch of the gate of Zion; the little Africas at his ears will not stop jing-a-ling.

> Duppy inna second-hand skin (duB/oom duB/oom)
> /Duppy inna second-hand skin.

The tune in his head layers over the syncopation of election bloodshed and hungry-belly outside. He pushes against the door, anxious to be about his father's business, but the years have not passed over and the density of the people's pain is so great, the door will not open.

FROM THE ANGEL'S LEDGER BOOK

[Abeng]

The invention of the clock has altered human pleasure. There are minutes and seconds in the day now, and not enough for love.

A little watch ticks in a man's trouser pocket on the floor. The angel stops the minute hand at 2:29 pm. The spider plant on the bedside table touches his lover's cheek.

Wind-day, 1759—The English clockmaker, J. Harrison, completes his design of the H-4 timepiece. It is built for seafaring and he intends to use it to measure longitude and map the world.

Portsmouth, November, 1761—William Harrison, records high-noon with his father's H-4, then boards the HMS Deptford and sets out for Jamaica. On board, a young cook is besotted with the captain's daughter. He makes her onion broth flavoured with wine from Madeira.

January 19, 1762—The Deptford arrives in Port Royal, Jamaica. Here, high-noon is balmy, the sea cloud-green; William records time while the cook finds carrots and tomatoes for the girl's soup. Meanwhile, the girl longs for William; William watches the sky.

The difference in high-noon between two points is the same as the difference in longitude between those points. The difference in longing between two people is the same as the difference in the taste of a salt tongue between two people. This is how maps of desire are charted. The mapmaker always makes history.

The invention of the clock has altered human navigation. Ships criss-cross the seas with ease, carrying grand pianos and chained slaves.

The line of longitude through Jamaica is measured at Port Royal: 76.8.

And what if the sea takes back her land?

HERE-SO; HALF WAY TREE

Fifth Day: Year of Stones

Vaughn disappears with the smoke and in the morning only her john-crow beads are left, scattered on the floor. The door cracks open easily now. What hath the years wrought? The air has the same dead-fruit smell, but there is a new madwoman guarding the clock. She holds a kitchen knife and stands perfectly still. In truth, it is not the clock she guards but the still-alive roots that agitate underground. Every cell in her foot-bottom feels; she smiles when a tingle thing travels up her legs. "Rah," she says soft, still watching the concrete.

Delroy is across the street setting up his banana chips, Cheese Krunchies and bottle drinks. Bob calls out to him and he turns with a wide, slice-breadfruit smile.

"I come to shine your shoes!" Bob says, and Delroy laughs. He has the same laugh of how-many years ago, only a little hoarser, like something catch up in his throat. "Is not joke I making; I come to shine your shoes," Bob says.

Babylon pushes through traffic with a blue-noise siren and the madwoman shifts the knife to her right hand.

"Big-up all madooman," says a breddren sitting on the curb.

Two schoolgirls step off a bus; each holds a spiral folder like a shield against her chest. The madwoman blinks away flies.

Duppy inna second-hand skin, Bob sings, and he stands at the curb and checks for his shoebrush and polish and soft-soft cloth. He takes out the radio and gives it to Delroy.

"It power with herb," he says. "Just put two spliff where the batteries go."

"Ah, Rastalogy for true." Delroy's eyes are bright like a small boy's.

"Ashe," whispers the woman with the knife. A young dread balances a stack of newspapers on his head. There's war and rumours of war on the front page—a boy in Trench Town points a gun at the camera; a girl behind him holds up her dolly. All day Bob wanders the streets of Kingston, meeting the eyes of the children, something in their voices—a ping—like gullybottom stones.

ATLANTIC LULLABY, 1790

[G Major]

There is a remembrance that goes this way:

One hundred and eighty-four slaves left on board the *Sarah*. Thirty-eight less than at departure from Calabar. They bring some of the sick ones on deck to wash them down. Dowse them with vinegar-water from a pail. The far-gone ones are made to jump overboard.

A child watches as her too-feverish mother is forced to jump. They lash her mother's legs to make her move. The whips make her feet dance the wet deck. Soon she is up against the stern, for there is nowhere else to go. The captain makes her straddle it; such long, dark legs. Like memory/

When the vessel leans to the side, the babymother dips/then flies/over the water—the green-blue parts/and covers her nakedness/for a moment/all silent/the sea mad mute.

When at last her head rises above, the child shrieks an alarm, sounding all the way to yet-to-come. Cold rain falls on the Atlantic, and a wind rushes in from the edge of the horizon. A sailor has arms quick as whips; he holds back the child with a firm grip. The others watch from the deck.

Iya? Mama! the girl-child calls, her legs kicking hard against the man's belly.

But by then, Iya is already washed away, far under the deepdeep, salt water in her lungs.

And she cannot hear.

KINGSTON RINGTUNE

There's a brown girl in the ring, tra-la-lala-la,
Brown girl in the ring, tra-la-lala-lala,

I was just seven when Daddy slap me because I couldn't read the time on the clock tower at Half Way Tree. He slap me up right in the middle of the square; I so shame. Everybody see him slap me on my face and everybody walk past and don't say a thing. I never know how to read Roman numerals is all; the numbers get me all mix-up. Why they have to put Roman numerals on the clock when we are not Roman? Sake of how Daddy slap me, I hate that clock. I wish it would drop down. I would like to smash it down. I still feel the slap-them on my face-and-arm-and-back-and-head. Big cocoa head, that's what him call me. Slow. Yu big and slow-like, him say. One day I going to throw a stone and smash that clock, I say.

Everyday I to get off the bus at Dunrobin, but today I get off at Half Way Tree because I come to smash the clock. I stand up under the lignum vitae, watching the minute hand, when I feel somebody touch my shoulder. I move quick because I don't want any madman touch me up. A man did touch up my cousin in the bus one day. The bus was pack and he put his hand in her skirt pocket and touch up her front that way. She take her pencil and jab him in the side and nobody never even know why him jump off the bus so quick a cuss. So I wasn't going to take no chance—I have three stones and if I don't smash the clock face, I smash his own.

But then the man say, I want to sing for you. And I know I not to answer no madman, but something in his voice sound kinda different, like him come from somewhere, not from foreign, but from somewhere don't have no name; so I say, What? And him say, I going to sing for you and when I sing, you going to see your face.

His locs tie up in a red scarf and he have two brass ears-ring that go ting-&-ting.

And him stand up straight and sing with a voice sound like it come out an ole-time radio, all scratch-up and far away. And I forget all about the clock and three stones in my hand, the man voice so—I don't know how to say it! His voice so dream-and-ting,

205

like I in a soft-breeze place full of fireflies—no, like my grand-moddah standing up in church in the spirit with her arms spread out, only is not church song the man singing—no, is Rasta song him singing, Rasta spirit tings, Rasta firefly, spirit tings. And I find myself start move to the bass, and his ears-rings shape-like-Africa justa move with me. And is the first time anybody sing me a song; nobody never sing for me-one. Is sunhot, but the fireflies turn on them lights and you know firefly light only supposed to turn on at night, and never in Kingston. Yes, me and the singing man in the square in a circle of little light-up tings, and Daddy can't reach through the firefly light to slap me no more; and it don't matter if I late for school, for is not true I slow. I look over the madman shoulder at the big clock and I know the time on every clock in every town in every country, for is only one time all of them have—and is now.

And the madman sing, You see your face? And I glimpse myself in his brass ears-rings, right in the middle of Africa, and I say, Yes, I see mi face; I see it.

She looks like a sugar and a plum, plum, plum,

Our moddah say the reason we are twins is because two man rape her one-time. How can two man rape you one-time? We don't want to know how that work. Our moddah say she take trouble and turn it into luck. Twins are luck. You must always take trouble and turn it into luckiness, she say. Still, when we see the madman coming, we wasn't going to trouble trouble. People call us the Bend-up Girls—that's because our two spine curve so bad we lean over to the side; one of us curve to the right and one curve to the left—we look like twisted trees. Our moddah said to turn twistback into blessing, just like when you take bitter cocoa and make it sweet, but we don't know how. At least you are not Siamese, she say. The two of us share one school bag between us; that way when one back start hurt, the other one takes it. Yu lucky! the one taking the bag says to the other.

So we on the street sharing a bag juice, when the madman say, You know there used to be a tree right where you standing? He have a smile on his face and even though he dress like madman, he don't sound like madman. His voice sound like it come from a storybook, the kind that you turn the page, and turn the page, and every word important. Before the clock tower, there was a tree, he say. They cut it down in 1912 to build the clock for an English king. Dig this. It was a powerful tree, silk cotton. Market people used to sit under it and catch their breath, and sake of that, the tree know plenty story. It know the sufferation of the people. And it know rejoicing too. The twist in the branches—you know where them come from? We shake our heads, No. Is when the tree dance with the sun, he say, Each twist it make, it become more beautiful.

The two of us, we look at each other and we look at the madman. He say, If you close your eyes, you can still feel the roots. Most people too rat race to close their eyes in Half Way Tree, but what a revelation if them would try.

We under his spell now, so we close our eyes; and we feel it, we feel it. Something trembling under the earth. Like a reggae vibe, it travel our back-bone, riff by riff, and when it get to our head-top we so shock, our eyes open quick—sound stretching us higher. The man still in front of us, standing there, smiling. Hold yu head up, he say. Feel Jah light. And he walk away and cross the street.

That night we tell our moddah about the man and the tree and the love thing that travel our back, and it make water come to her eye. She cover her pot and hold us, and then she sit at the kitchen table and make us earrings shape like Africa. She carve them from coconut shell that throw outside, and she polish-polish till we see our face in it. When she hook them on our ears she say, Even coconut trash can turn blessing.

Show me yu motion, tra-la-lala-la,

See me here standing at the bus stop and I don't really want to go to school because I was too hungry last night to study my seven times, and today Miss going to make us recite it. Government say not to beat us, but Miss have a ruler and sometimes, if you don't careful, you feel it sting your shoulder. I have a play-play gun in my school bag. It look real, and come recess, I going to shoot myself with it.

Anyway, I standing at the bus stop thinking on the gun, when a man bend down and start clean my shoes; quick-time I move and say, What yu doing? And he say, Just cool, and he take out a brush and start shine my shoes, same-so, like is that he born for. He look up at me and say, Seven is a number in Jahrithmetic. And is like he read my mind and know all my worries, just like that. The brush have some bristles that massage under my skin, and he shine and shine and I don't want him stop, for each time him move the brush is like me make from the number seven, every little bit of me come in sevens.

Seven is the number of greatness, him say. And me feel the number seven justa multiply inside me, pass seven times everyting and is like me going on too; the numbers can't stop. No end to the number seven, no end to my greatness, an ever-sound that tremble like an electric guitar string.

Seven is the number of greatness, the man say again. You feel how great you is? And the greatness don't stop. It justa multiply and multiply and it go all the way out to a place don't have no edge, and that make from the same thing that sound make from. Where belly-laugh come from, and music, and baby cry. I start to cry too, and the cry turn into a laugh and the laugh can't stop; it just multiply like the sevens. And when the man finish shine my shoes, the little maps at his ears jing-a-ling on and on like a dub ting; and he say, *That's how great you is.*

I late, but I go to school in time for Miss and her seven times drill. Miss call on everybody one-one and when she get to me, she point with her ruler and say, Seven times seven? And I say, Forty-nine, Miss. Miss, do you know the number seven is the number of greatness? For by now, I can carry seven to the place of Jahrithmetic. For is like I fill with more than stars in the sky. And is like the good thing I fill with can't stop; it go on and on and I know all the numbers; I just counting them like lucky Jack sevens. My uncle is a Seventh Day Adventist, but their seven don't multiply; it stop and start, stop and start again. This seven go on and on like a cup of water that have no bottom, like shine tings in the sky that can't count, like a pomegranate that can never run out of seeds—every time you spit one out, you find more; like playing in soap water and the bubbles coming up, coming up. I get to find me is the number seven, multiplied over and over, no end to me, no stopping me, and no matter what Miss ask, is me the number, me the factor, me the product, me the answer.

Miss coming back down the row of desks and when she get to me again she say, Seven times twelve? And I say, Eighty-four. Then I look at her and say, But Miss, eighty-four really too small for how great I am and how great you is. And Miss look at me like she want faint and she say, But Jesus.

Show me yu motion, tra-la-lala-la,

[Schoolgirl Queen]

The principal say not to dance and whine up yourself on the street when we in school uniform. Hem your skirt at least two inches below the knee, she say. And no long nails look like claws. But the principal can't control we. Them put we in this uniform like a straight-jacket because them want control we. Them fraid of sex-iness; them fraid it jump out on them. My two titty so ready to push out, the buttons on my blouse straining. You are over-ripe for your age, my auntie say. Sit with your legs closed. Force-ripe, girl, she say.

I wait at the bus stop a listen Lady She, when a madman go, Pssst. I think he psst me because I sexy, so I don't pay him no mine. I just keep listening Lady She. I want practice move my hip like hers, like a wheel inside it. This weekend I going over Juanita house to touch up my hair roots and afterwards the two of we will practice. This is when I remember I need go York Pharmacy to get some Revlon. I wish I could get a weave, but school rules don't al-low it. Pssst, the madman go again. Kiss my raas, I say, and I cross the street and walk over to the pharmacy.

When I come out and go back to the bus stop, he's still there. I hold my head straight and make sure I stand far away, but he walk to where I am and sit down on the curb behind me. I want to touch up yuh roots, he say. And his words shock me because the Revlon in my school bag, so how he could know? No. Maybe is just because my roots so nappy and him notice—but still! Or maybe he have a nasty mouth.

I just ignore him and I look down the street like I watching for the bus. You need to touch yuh roots, he say again. And when I don't say nothing, him start to hum and I move away again because I still listening Lady She in my ears, and I visioning how her two knees touch and part, touch and part. I like when she sing, Hell-o, just as they about to part.

Someone calling my cell. But the madman still won't leave me.

He move up gainst the fence and he still humming. I kiss my teeth and take Lady She out my ears, and then is like his voice vibrate the ground under my feet. I feel it on my foot-bottom, like something under the ground reaching up through my skin. And then the roots on my head start tingle. I touch my scalp, so nappy like a forest my fingers get lost in it. I circle the top where my auntie said my tender spot used to be when I was born. The hair coily and soft there and I remember something—my mother holding me when I was a baby. Who remembers their mother holding them when them was a baby? Shit, you not supposed to remember that far back, but something about the madman and his humming make me remember it. I have my head against her chest and she singing a song. Is a Bob Marley song. My mother always used to like Bob Marley. She was young when she had me and went abroad when I was four years old; I believe American cares-of-life swallow she, because she don't come back since. Is my auntie I grow with. But my head against my mother's chest now, and she smell like nutmeg sprinkle on milk and I close my eyes and see something else, clear-clear: my mother in *her* mother's arms—my grandmother, the small bird-woman, holding my mother so proud, and a fire tears-drop on her cheek, and in the tears-drop I see the bird-woman in *her* mother's arms—my great-grandmother, the strong-back maroon woman, and the picture in our tears just keep going back and back to all of us in our mother's arms and on and on, can't stop, all of us with the same tender spot at the top of our heads and all of us thinking of the ones before us; the heat in our tears, like we are one woman.

My bus coming down the road, but I stand there with my fingers in my roots, so much baby laugh and gurgle coming up from inside me, and the hair so twist and spiral around, and the man behind me humming like a prophet. Ti-ting-ting, his earrings blow in the breeze, as I coil my roots around my finger. And I love them, I love them. And I wonder if Lady She ever feel that way.

She looks like a sugar and a plum, plum, plum,

Today Grade Three in the school yard playing ring games when fight break out. The game was going alright when all of a sudden Minerva say, Hold on, and she stop the game. She say we missing a verse. Is not so the song go, she say. Minerva always want everything perfect and Renita can't stand it, or maybe is just Minerva voice tick her off, I don't know. Anyway, Renita say, Shut up yu know-all, Minerva. And watch how you want bring bwoy in the game too. Is a girl game, and the boys don't let us in their games. Minerva say, Well the game nicer when it have plenty people. Just let the boys play. Everyone know we have more sense than them, so maybe they will learn something to rah. The whole time the boys on the side watching. All you have to do is call us brown boys, Peter say. Peter grow with him granny, Owen say. And then Susan Chin say, There's something I don't like. Is a brown game. What if some of us are not brown? Shut up! All of us brown, Minerva say. Even you, Susan. Look how sun burn you. And anyway, is just a song. Except Sharon, she black-like, Nadine say. That's when Sharon box Nadine in her face and soon the ring game turn ring fight—Sharon and Nadine in the middle.

The whole time a man at the fence watching us. Him have on a red turban and look like him travel from far. Renita whisper, Don't look at him because he's mad and if you look at him he will cross your face and you will die. The man wind-pipe have a guitar in it, and he sing a song that shake the leaves on the tamarind tree, and right away the fight stop, and everyone turn around and look at him, and all the green tamarind fall down. Even teacher come to the door.

I go teach you a new game, the man say. Get back in the circle, he say. Everybody look at each other, and we get back in the circle. For what there was to lose? We already look him in the face. Close your eyes, he say. This feel like church, Owen say. The man laugh and his earrings go ting-ling-ting. For this game, we need one person in the circle, he say. Minerva step forward; she is always good that way. She put her hands over her eyes and shut them, just like he tell her, and he start hum.

When I close my eyes, I see my mother washing clothes in the yard, Minerva say. She washing yuh panty, Owen say. Everybody start giggle, but Minerva all serious. She want to give me a number 11 mango, Minerva say. Take it, the man say. And Minerva take the mango and taste it and you could hear a stone drop because all of us taste it too, sweet-sweet like only number 11 can taste, and true like the soft thing in Minerva mother heart. Everybody get a turn in the ring. Sharon go next and her grandfather give her piece of black cloth with a new moon in it.

She unfold it and we feel the night on our skin, because each one of us turn a star in it.

Susan's auntie give her a red ginger lily. Ginger Lily beautiful everywhere it grow, her auntie say. She say it in Chinese, but we understand, because we are all holding hands.

A man Owen don't know give him a cut-in-half calabash. He put the calabash to his ears and we hear a soft singing, like how you sing to a newborn baby. Owen's father singing a just-born song to his son, all bass and loveful, and Owen start cry because is the first he hear his father voice.

When my turn come, my mother give me a needle and piece of blue thread. As I thread the needle and look through the eye, I see all the way across the sea to an old-old woman with long white plaits, holding out a page with my voice on it. My name is Zion she say, and we all walk on the salt water towards her.

Skip across the ocean, tra-la-lala-la
Skip across the ocean, tra-la-lala-lala
Skip across the ocean,

Is three of us in the lane. We find a dead bird and we want roast it—bird meat is the sweetest meat. We push at it with a twig; the eyes and the beak still open and we slide it in a scandal bag. The plan was to roast the bird and eat it, and then slap up the girl at the shack shop on the corner and make her give us three sodas. She is a fool-fool slut and we like to do her that way. That's when we hear a voice behind us. The voice say, Mine that bird. We turn around and is a funny-looking Rastaman—maybe he mad too—with a red turban and two map earrings and a carve-up rod. Rhaatid, don't be Rasta *and* mad.

He grab the bag from us, like he rule over it and he say, Mine you eat yuh next of kin.

And who talk like that to bloodclaat? The three of us have knives in our pockets, not just for the bird, but for anyone who need swipe up. And we would cut this man too to raas. We stab an old man in his eye one time, just for so—for practice. He bawl, and a thick, slow blood ooze out the cut; and we make our self watch.

So the three of us reaching in our back pocket now, when the Rasta hold up his two hands and say, Stop that thought. And is not what him say that make us stop, is his hands—he don't have no lines on them. Them blank like a lineless paper.

How old you is? him say.

Ten and eleven and eleven, we want say, but we can't say it. The words won't come.

You young enough to know better, him say. And the whole time we watching the two hands—how big them is—one of them with a ring that glint.

You remember times of slavery? him say.

But we can't answer because is like when you in a dream and no sound come out yuh throat.

You remember times of slavery? him say again, louder this time.

And one of us mumble, No Ras.

Well yu should remember, him say, Because you still in it.

Then he start hum a tune, an old-time Bob Marley tune, and is like him voice is a soundtrack. We all know the words—*Emancipate yourself.* He still holding up his hands, and now a flim showing on them, a double-screen flim. There's a ship crossing sea, and three boys on it, look like us, but chain to each other. And then the scene change and the three boys in a cane field, and there's a girl too— with one-cent skin, like the shack shop girl. She holding her belly and she ready to drop down, and she turn around and mouth, *Help me,* to the camera, like she know we watching, standing in the lane from four hundred years away. And the scene change again and the girl leaving quick in the night. And this time she don't look in the camera; her eyes watch the ground. Later, the three boys tell which way she run and the whiteman give them salt pork and they chew on it and drink rain water, and the whiteman get his horse and dogs. Two grey hounds with tails like whips.

There's barking. The flim on the Rasta hands goes blank, and when we look over his shoulder, a girl, running toward us—is the shack shop girl—and a dog chasing behind her. She have that same-same look in her eyes, *Help me.* And we taste salt pork in our mouth. And we spit it out.

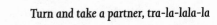

Turn and take a partner, tra-la-lala-la

[Singing Boy]

I hate school; I hate that concrete drill sergeant place, and I not going there today. And I hate my yard too; I hate the tough mattress in the corner, and the sirens that go *whoo whoo* in the night. Every time you hear a siren, you know somebody else dead. I know a place where I can go, though—here under the stinking-toe tree, making a song; I like how it feel when I belt it out. When I grow up I want to be a musician. I am going to go to a recording studio and record a song. My song will be a kinda reggae, kinda dancehall, kinda rebel, kinda gangsta song. I'm not sure what I will call it yet, but it will have a name. Or maybe it don't need a name. I like it when the Rastas flash their locs; it look like freedom, so maybe I'll get locs, long ones that sweep the air. I like dancehall and the nice dancehall girls too; I like their long legs in crisscross stocking; though sometimes when the words so slack, I shame to sing in front my mother; she watch me from her corner-eye. But them girls can dance though.

So, I under the stinking-toe tree minding my own business, making up a song when a Rasta man come and sit beside me. I think he mad, but I not sure. I want to teach you to chant down Babylon, he say. He little bit different, but I not scared because he have kindness in his eye.

Sing, he say. And I sing, Whoo concrete and sugar-and-wata tears; and he sing with me and we both know all the words, the two of us making them up together. We stay under the stinking-toe and make a drum from a turn-over bucket, and we chant down Babylon and every badness in it. He know what sufferation is, this man. We chant down guns/and wata/lock-off/and electric city bill/and hungry belly/and the padlock that keep/my faadah/my faadah/my faadah in jail.

And after that, we sing a freedom that take up the whole sky and the whole air, and a whole sea and all the fish in the sea and all the sand at the bottom and the whole of the whole of it.

You feel alright?

Yes, I say. And I know something now too. I know where Zion is, I say.

Is a place inside, he say. Keep it close and carry on, he say.

[WE, JAH-JAH CHILDREN]

For we are the madman children. Who knows how many of us there is? But if each of us shine seven children shoes and each of those children shine seven more; soon we will have a whole army. And if each of us sing seven songs and each of those seven songs reverb in the four directions of the four faces of Half Way Tree, we will have a whole choir. Jahrithmetic does multiply that way. Turn and take a partner, tra-la-lala-la-la. And if each of us tell seven stories and each of those seven stories fly, tearing full speed off the pages of our spiral books, the sky over Kingston will resound with such a twittering, even the Prime Minister, no, even Mr. Barack Obama-self with his good all-lined-up-in-a-row teeth, will have to listen, tra-la. So help us, Jah.

A girl is reading a book at a bus stop on Hagley Park Road. Bob knows her face now—pretty, with pimples on the forehead, which she picks as she reads; each day, she is the only one who never changes. Always the same age, and always rapt in the pages, only her hair and clothes different. This time she wears a T-shirt with words: *Here-so.*

"Tomorrow is my last chance," he says.

She turns a page as if she does not hear him.

"Yu find I&I name yet?"

He begins to sing, but that does not work on this dawta. She blinks and turns another page. A bus comes, but she does not get on it. A fly pitches on her eye-lid, but she does not brush it away. And then, the clock at Half Way Tree chimes. Who would think it could chime? The girl looks up in the direction of the square. It is six o'clock.

"What yu name?"

"They call me Red Ear," she says. "I spell it the Jahlexic way."

hear this; hear this:
the rain it a fall it a fall/the wind it a blow it a blow/
is a anti-clock wind
wise-up yu-self
revolution deh ya quick-quick
quick/

HOUSE OF ZION

ADDIS ABABA, 1972
MEHARENE

The Imperial Apartment [Version]

Me and the sweeper, the mute Jamaican, were the only ones allowed in the emperor's apartments. To change the sheets, remove the laundry and dust the furniture was my job. Immediately after His Majesty left, I was to take care of these chores.

Each morning, I waited beside the door as I was not allowed to enter until H.I.M. departed. When his door opened finally, I stood to the side and looked down at the floor, for to look H.I.M. barefaced in the eye, I dared not. He was an early riser and liked to walk mornings in the garden. As soon as he left I stripped the bed and spread clean linen, left fresh pyjamas on top the pillow. I had received explicit instructions to fold the pyjamas with the buttons undone, the shirt placed on top of the trousers. His bed slippers were to be put on the east side of the bed. The pyjamas always blue, ordered from London, and his matching bathrobes had silk collars and little breast pockets in which I found sometimes peppermints or a Vicks inhaler. Such items I left on the bedside table, always. Sometimes from the upstairs window I glimpsed H.I.M. down in the garden. He was a lonely figure, there among the hibiscus, his only companion a little dog. Chihuahua, very loyal dog.

The whole time I clean, the Jamaican waited by the door, as I was never allowed in apartment alone. As soon as I finished strip the bed, he swept the room with great ceremony. Was there a school somewhere in Jamaica for rooms sweeping? I had never seen it done that way. I paused at the door and watched him, his broom like an instrument of consecration, no corner left unsanctified—seventy times seven. And the bed—under it and around, in one direction and then the other—and after that, the ceiling. At the end of it all, he bowed his head and was gone.

Before I came to Jubilee Palace, my mother worked here. We are from a family of goat herders and her employment by Empress Menen was a great honour. She became the empress's personal assistant in all things domestic. It was my mother who packed the empress's clothes—nineteen trunks full—when she died. The empress had two hundred and twenty-eight pairs of shoes, ninety-two brassieres, a hundred and four pairs of knickers, forty-nine petticoats, twenty-six pairs of gloves, sixty-seven handkerchiefs and perfume enough to scent the wrists of every woman in Ethiopia. One afternoon, as my mother sorted and put away, a note fell from a feather slipper.

Dearest Tafari,

A lion ought not lose his whiskers so easily.

She pushed the note in her brassiere and took it home. From then on, the emperor's whiskers the subject in our family of many jokes.

Mother worked for the emperor until she was fifty-seven; then one day her heart gave out and they sent instead for me. I was nineteen and worked there sixteen years. To attend to His Majesty's linen, wardrobe and personal effects was my job. He demanded cleanliness and order. In its place, every pin.

One morning, as I waited the emperor to leave the room, he remained inside unusually long. Finally, just a crack the door opened. I heard shuffling about the room and thought I heard "Come," but to look inside I was too afraid. Later the emperor left in his usual manner and I cleaned the room and wondered. It was just a small thing, but the emperor was a man so predictable in his habits. The Jamaican showed no sign of noticing anything at all. He consecrated the four-poster bed, tapped his broom three times at the threshold, then locked the door. That was the other thing about the sweeper—he was the only servant entrusted with keys to the apartment.

The next day, as he left, H.I.M. paused and said, "Meharene." I stepped back a little against the wall; that the emperor even knew my name I had not been aware. He handed me, on a black string, a little brass prayer pendant. His eyes were kind and when he smiled, I saw between his teeth there was a gap. I knew the emperor was not one to give away easily such smiles.

The prayer necklace marked the beginning of my relationship with Haile Selassie. On mornings, when the door was cracked, I knew that I was to enter the room before he left, then take off my shoes and remove my apron. He had slender fingers and long nails that he grazed against my skin. He liked me to smother him with silk bed pillows—just a little—before he had to come up for air, laughed and needed to put in his nose the Vicks inhaler. The emperor was austere in public, but now I knew why he had been forewarned about the danger of losing whiskers. Gradually I began to arrive earlier; the door cracked oftener. Once we listened to Billie Holiday in bed and he showed me, behind his ear, the place where by a magpie in his youth he had been pecked. The magpie had been attracted to the shiny hoop in his ear. It left with a piece of his skin instead. Understand I enjoyed these forays with the emperor. It gave me special privilege, true, but then much later, I also loved him.

Always the Jamaican waited patiently outside, sweeping afterwards with his usual fervour. I was glad he was mute. They called him "Rasta," and it was rumoured that his people took the emperor for god; I wondered at his surprise at the capers of god. His presence outside the door made episodes in the emperor's bedchamber all the more interesting. With god I liked cavorting. Once, as I clipped H.I.M.'s beard, I asked, "What will the Jamaican of his god think now?" H.I.M. got up and closed the curtains, stood for a while and said this: "Who among us is god enough to choose to whom another man should pray?" For a long time I thought on those words, of their meaning not sure.

When came the Dergue, I filled the prayer box with supplication. I prayed to every blade benevolent of grass, drop of rain, piece of moon; and with every fibre of my being, for His Majesty's safety, so help me god.

ADDIS ABABA: WHAT THE SWEEPER SAW

3rd Version I-witness

Outdoors, H.I.M. pulled himself to his full height (for he was not a tall man) and walked in the garden, so confident in his stride no one would have guessed the peril in his empire. He paused at an angel's trumpet flower, stood with trademark posture, back straight, his fingers pressed together—thumb to thumb and index to index. Over the years, poets had called this space of his hands a consecrated heart, the holy of holies, a crown jewel. But it was Riva Man, chanting down Anansi web from the west window, who paused one morning and saw Jah truth—H.I.M. walking in the palace garden carrying the heart of Africa, careful as a high priest.

He saw that the Most High carried Zion for groundation and protection; for I-liverance and remembrance; for the alpha and omega of her she-lion roar. He saw that he loved Africa and would give his life for her.

In the cool of the morning, the Most High, looking up from the garden, saw Riva Man silent at the window, and though no words passed between them, their eyes made four—hibiscus pollen dropping libation on the path.

RIVA MAN

Twelve-Corner Stream of Reasoning

I&I sanctify this chamber this day. Let no badminded-ness enter therein. Jah live.

Rasta-far-eye in the east/Rasta-far-eye in the west/Rasta-far-eye in the north/Rasta-far-eye in the south/Rasta-far-eye above/Rasta-far-eye below. Jah live.

Holy holy are His Majesty's feet/His Majesty's hands/His Majesty's head/His Majesty's liver/His Majesty's heart/His Majesty's lungs/His Majesty's loins/Jah Live.

I&I guard and I&I protect His Majesty's bed, and the sheets which cover him. Sanctify the four-poster feet that touch the ground as lion's paws.

Rasta-far-eye sees—Jah-Jah maidservant/her woman spleen/her woman ovaries/her woman kidneys/her woman hands that fold/that fold/the sheets; and hold the blue love pillow/over Jah-Jah joyful face. When the time comes, may her lips stay sealed/her eyes keep their secrets.

I&I knew/a woman with eyes like that/amber bottle-glass. Vaughn. Her name was Vaughn. Her locs were one hundred and forty-four. The last she spoke, I heard from under the window/she said these words: Jah live.

Jah live and I&I count his name I-tinually as I sweep and I-tinually as I walk and I-tinually as I breathe and

bass and fortify and bless the spider in the corner, for the broom breaks her house, but still she returns; she will not be moved. She builds her temple in the small hours of the morning; and even the prayers of the Most High resound therein.

Jah live in the east/Jah live in the west/Jah live in the north/Jah live in the south/Jah live above/Jah live below/and above-above and below-below; for His ways are the ways of oneness.

I&I sweep to guard and protect the red-red curtains that cover the shadow of/the shadow of/the shadow of Jah/from falling words.

But how do you pray for the Almighty? I&I pray to Jah to remember himself and not forsake himself.

Selah in the east/and in the west/selah in the north/and in the south/selah above and below.

Jah live.

MEHARENE

Last Rite

They hated His Majesty. "Ethiopia is starving," they said. "He feeds his lions choice meat while the people starve. Look at our children, their bellies bloated from starvation. Our women wearing skin and bone. What good is the blood of Solomon and Makeda to us now? Dynasty cannot feed the hungry. Dynasty cannot clothe the naked. Dynasty cannot save our sick." The rebel students were the worst. "Die nasty," they said in foul English. "Down with the emperor!"

The Dergue. They infiltrated the palace right under His Majesty's nose. No one he could trust. Like slender razors in his side they were, opening a vein, sucking his blood. One day one of the lions was found poisoned. Then one by one the servants and dignitaries disappeared. There were rumours the Dergue enjoyed murder by strangulation best. A high-ranking minister locked in a dungeon was left to starve. Each person watched the other, even flesh and blood could not be trusted. H.I.M. did nothing. He was like lamb to the slaughter. Who could he turn to? He was surrounded by enemies. The military, the ministers, the servants—everyone had bloody hands, it seemed.

Me, he trusted. He trusted me. That last morning in his apartment, he read me a psalm of his ancestor, David; then fearful for my life, begged me to leave. He said I was Africa and Africa should be free.

BACKGROUND SINGER SOUND SISTREN [SISTAH MAUVA]

Track 14.0: Bobo Infrasound

Not a living soul spoke to Riva Man and Riva Man spoke to not a one.

He was a keeper of secrets, the keeper of the keys, the keeper of the Most High.

He swept the pathway clear-clear of stones so that when His Majesty walked with the heart of Africa out in the garden he would not slip nor fall.

But for the love of power, bad-mindedness shall abound. People started to su-su su-su. They looked at the quiet man with the brooms and iniquity filled them up and one morning when he was gathering the thatch, they way-lay him and beat him and throw him out in the street and that's when the downpressors close in on the Most High.

The day news break say the Most High dead, Riva Man tongue catch afire and he ran through the streets of Addis Ababa shouting, "Bloodfiah! Bloodfiah!" Nobody in Jamaica in the little district of Priory in the garden parish of St. Ann knew a thing, but hear this, mongoose and dog did holler that night.

FROM THE ANGEL'S LEDGER BOOK

[Handmade Acoustic/Sardine Can Guitar]

The Emperor's maidservant is pregnant. She is comely like Mariam in his youthful dream.

H.I.M. attributes his virility to walks in the garden and the company of lions.

At the moment of the child's conception, H.I.M. remembers Les Vingt et Un, and recites them in Meharene's ear. This memory of words renders him as a young man.

Only the mute Jamaican hears the sounds from under the door. And the angel. The angel listens too.

The Dergue prods H.I.M. for secrets—keys to safeboxes, Swiss account numbers, the whereabouts of relics and jewels, hidden tunnels underground. They listen as he talks in his sleep. "Meharene," he says. But in the morning H.I.M. keeps his mouth sealed; he will not be moved. All secrets go with him to the grave, including Les Vingt et Un.

They throw his body in the sewer. The baby in the maidservant's womb sucks her little hoof.

MEHARENE

Version: The Scent of Peppermint

I was the one who killed the Most High. Three soldiers came for me in the night, dragged me out of bed and into his room pushed me. One of them tore the prayer box from my neck. They stripped my clothes off and took my bangles. All these years, and I had never shown H.I.M. my nakedness. Even when we lay in bed together I always kept my clothes on.

His Majesty was stretched on a cot by a window. Someone had been kicking him—on his skin there were black and blue marks. He looked at me and I saw on his face the aloneness. I began to cry. They gave me his pillow—it was one of the silk blue ones from the imperial apartment. Of blood and urine and the entrails of a small animal, it smelled. They wanted me to suffocate him.

"I won't do it!" I said.

One of them put a gun to my back and when I still refused, they began to beat me. "Ça suffit!" H.I.M. called and he made as if to get up but was quickly struck down by a club. They left me on the tile floor, too weak to move. A soldier chewing khat, spat it in my face. I held the pillow against me, buried my face into it, a life-line.

When I was a small girl, I fell on a cactus once; the thorns stuck in both my hands. My sister the only one home and she ran to help me, but I would let no one else pull the thorns except grandmother. Eight hours I waited until grandmother came home. She had been all day at the market and smelled of goat's milk; I buried my head under her arm and shut my eyes tight. I trusted her each thorn to curse as she pulled it out. Seventeen she counted. When grandmother turned old, her womb fell down and poke sometimes between her legs; it happen to women that age. My job to bath it and push it back in each time, and each time she cry for her eight children who grow there, seven of them dead before her, my mother except. Life give us job—when my mother dead, my job to tell grandmother the news. I want to tell grandmother before the neighbours do. I bath grandmother and wash her womb with salt water, and fold a eucalyptus leaf inside, then push it back in. I never said a word; but the news, she know it. Many years after and I talk this part later—my sister job to pull a sorrow-nail from my heart. It bleed for a little while, but after that, the sorrow stop. Suffering, I know. I know suffering.

So as I lay on the tile, the thought arrive to me—they were going to kill H.I.M. anyway—that perhaps it would be best if I am the one to do the deed. Life give us job.

At my back, again a gun clicked. "Your love pillow; take it!" said the soldier. I pulled the pillow against me and crawled to the cot where His Majesty lay. His breathing was shallow and great effort he had to exert when he spoke.

"I only am left," he said.

The soldier moved close behind, chewed his khat; green saliva he spat at my feet.

"Move it, your gun." I said.

And I don't know—perhaps because the khat made him giddy— he took the gun from my back, stood quiet by the wall.

I kissed H.I.M. behind the ear where the magpie stole his skin, and I whispered words I heard the Jamaican say. *Jah live.* Those words, I like them. They mean, I think, something good for H.I.M. They are the only words the sweeper says. *Jah live Jah live.* H.I.M. closed his eyes then, because he understood. I held the pillow over his head, and did not let go.

HERE-SO; HALF WAY TREE

The Red Ear Girl

"A lunch money for this ring," Bob says.

He takes the ring out of the toilet paper and holds it out for the girl to see. She takes it and turns it over, runs her thumb over the lion.

"I look like I have money to you?" She gives it back.

"Then tell me my true name then. I'll give you it for my true name."

She tilts her head as if watching for birds, takes back the ring and rests it in the crease of her book.

"Alright," she says. And she closes the book with the ring still inside; walks away without a word down Hagley Park Road.

MEHARENE

Aftermath

I lay there for a while, my head on top of the pillow. No one moved. Somewhere a bell rang. Just a small sound—like a bell on a girl's ankle bracelet. I wanted to stay that way, to die right there with him. To die, it would have been a good moment. This, the finale of all I had been born for.

I lifted the pillow. There was a smile on H.I.M.'s face as if he was in the middle of a lovely dream. The scent of peppermint filled the room and one of the soldiers shaken from stupor crossed the room; I looked him in the eye and felt no fear. The scamps, they were nervous suddenly now, impatient to get rid of the body. One put his gun to my neck, but the others said, "No." They thought I knew His Majesty's secrets and did not want to kill me yet.

To this day I wonder. How could the Dergue have known about the silk pillows? The Jamaican was the only one who knew of our games. He also had the keys to the imperial apartment. But even then, the door had always remained closed as he waited outside. Perhaps it was all just coincidence. I don't believe the Jamaican betrayed. This I don't think.

I had H.I.M.'s baby. A little girl named N. born with one foot like a goat. No one knew she was H.I.M.'s child, not even she. When she grew and asked for her father, I told her he was killed in the Red Terror. "You have his long nose and arching eyebrows," I say. "And his smile. You have his smile." The truth is, I have guarded her identity like a secret in a shroud.

My sister was the one who delivered N. She said, Push, and I pushed with all my might, something furious. N. was coming legs

244

first and we were worried for her safety. I squeezed the edge of the bed, too weak to push anymore. At the church across the way, a priest was shaking a tambourine. When I pushed again, something made my sister scream.

In silence my sister bathed N., wrapped her in a cloth then put her in my arms. "Throw her away," she said, "before it is too late." But I was already holding the little hoof in my hand.

News of the hoof spread like grassfire. Some days the children say I mated with a goat, some days it is a hyena. I like it best when they say lion. I tell N. to be proud of her hoof.

*

Today, twenty-two years later, she leaves for Addis Ababa. She goes to study in the university there; she will be great woman. This I believe. We wait by the road for a truck to take her to town. The driver, we know him, and N. sits in front with her suitcase. I want to say, *Jah live*, but I keep it inside. My sister and me, we watch the truck leave, standing at the dusty edge of the earth, two women. Then, this is how my sister redeems us, pulls the nail from my heart—

"The Queen of Sheba, she had one too," she says.

There is a sound. In the wind, eucalyptus leaves.

"Return is in the blood," I say.

I write the word *eucalyptus* in the dust with my finger. I like the look of that word, like the curves of a wrought-iron pattern in an open gate.

Revelation of Wisdom According to Jah Prophet (0:52)

[7.83 Hz]

(A woman on her way to town catches a shadow from her corner eye—a quick dance of yellow light from a hole in a cotton tree's trunk. She stops, puts out her spliff, goes behind the fence, bends close to better look. The tree parts its legs, the hole at its base growing larger; the smell—damp earth, goat's pee-pee and broken sparrow eggs. The woman sprinkles a little wisdom weed inside the opening, realizing that with effort she can fit her whole body within, the space widening to accommodate her shoulders, her hips, the length of her thighs, her bare feet. When at last she opens her eyes, she is in a womb lit up with fireflies; honey-yellow sap travelling up and down the walls. The womb grows larger, fireflies dancing a spiral above her head, the alive sap reasoning with revelation buttercup pollen and soldier ants underground. As she blinks to adjust to firefly light, she hears a voice, *Zion*, and at that moment, she is filled with yellow, the light washing off her heart, settling in the empty bowl of her belly-bottom, warming her tail-bone. By the time she climbs outside, the bus into town has already gone, but what does it matter?

She takes her spliff from behind her ear, lights it and continues on down the road.)

HERE-SO; HALF WAY TREE

Light Rain

That night, there is sobbing in the clock tower. Bob sits on the ground, feels a tear fall on his cheek; it is not his—it comes from somewhere above his head. He wipes it off with the back of his sleeve and another tear falls and then another and soon there is a light rain falling from the rafters. Outside it is windy. A howling, bearing many-year news. The debris circling the tower is mixed with old bullets and bits of dry placenta, backbiting and confusion and blue lignum vitae flowers and sighing and dogs barking and milk teeth and the mud of funeral shoes and music. Just as suddenly as the wind starts, it stops. And so does the sobbing. Bob opens his eyes and sees a small whiteman sitting up in the rafters. He is holding a baby bird in his hand. The bird tweets and pecks at his palm.

"I died in 1955 of a weak heart," the man says. "My heart stopped at 1:19 a.m. in the morning. The moon was waning and I had grey socks on."

Bob rubs his beard. The man's eyes are little watery puddles. He sniffs and takes a hanky out of his shirt pocket and blows his nose.

"It would have been better to die with a waxing moon," the man says. And then with a quick smile—"The astrology of the dead, you know."

Bob is quiet. The white hands holding the chick are shaking. He knows those hands. He knows the feel of them, clammy and hot against his.

"Is you them call Norval?"

RASTAMAN

Rhaatid

Check this. I look in the white man face and is like I&I see meself.
Rhaatid. Me, Bob Marley, see meself in the little white man face.
Is like me looking on meself, only is a white man me looking on. I
turn me head one-side, because me couldn't face it, Rasta. Is true
me talk one love and justice for all; and is true Jah no partial, but
that day inna the clock tower when me see meself in the white
man face, me frighten. How his structure match my structure.
Down to his foot-bottom same as mine. But hear me now—him
never recognize me; because me inside the Fall-down skin.

"I had a son once," Norval says. "His name was Nesta. The last time I saw him he was five years old—a little half-caste boy. I was a bloody coward and I gave him away. As I left him at the gate, I felt his eyes—like red ants on my back. But I kept on going. Back to my mother's house."

The bird in Norval's palm falls asleep and he puts it in his shirt pocket.

"If I could do it again, I would keep the boy. But that was 1951."

The bird chirps and sticks its head out.

"Me glad you never keep the boy. He would turn fool. Like you," Bob says.

Norval wipes his eyes and looks away. Someone outside pees against the door; it is warm and musty inside the clock. There is a sound up in the rafters like the murmuring of a congregation. Feet shuffling. Bob looks up, peering at cobwebs.

"They say one time there was a cotton tree in this place, right where we stand. Cotton tree harbour duppy; them draw dead like a magnet. Is my grandfather, Omeriah, tell me that. Omeriah—that man was a healer. And a conqueror." Bob gives Norval a sideways look.

At Omeriah's name, Norval starts to cry—like a small boy, wringing his eyes with his hands.

NORVAL

Jamaica Whiteboy; 1887

(The piano is black with white teeth. Mother keeps the lid closed. A mouse lives inside it; I feed it cheese.)

*

Mother, is it true that Great-grandmother was *a* black woman, black *as the Ace of Spades?* Where did you get that? Keep your bloody mouth shut. I don't want to ever hear you ask that again. Well, is it true *that the Ace of Spades was a great black grandmother?* Norval! But I asked *something different* –

*

We are English from Sussex.

*

(and white with black teeth.) and mother, why did we get a piano if no one can even play it? Can we fix it, Mother? Pleaseplease? Can we? You promised –

*

(My mother has *a* silent piano. The piano has *a* silent mother. The silent mother has *a* piano. The silent piano has no mother. The silent piano needs tuning. We are an out of tune family. There is no family in this tune. This family needs tuning.)

*

Mother, last night I dreamed of a boy. He looked just like me, except he had a dark face and knotty hair. Where do you get all this bloody nonsense? Nowhere, mother.

*

The thing you need to understand is this: We are rare birds on this island.

*

(The doctor bird is a rare species of hummingbird found only in Jamaica. Jamaica is full of a rare species of humming. The rare bird is humming. The humming doctor bird is a rare bird. Humming birds are rare doctors. A rare bird is the humming doctor bird. Rare birds like that are in fact common. There is no humming in this rare family. Humming in this family is rare. This rare family does not hum.)

*

Norval, why are you crying? A girl laughed and called me whiteboy. You are too soft, Norval. Soft boys do not survive on this island. Stop the foolish crying. You have to let these people understand who you are. Whiteboys like you have rights. Exercise your rights.

*

(Whiteboys exercise rights on this island. This island exercises white boys' rights. Rights on this island are a whiteboy's exercise. White rights are exercised on this island. This family has white right boys. I am a whiteboy.)

"There is a recording which plays over and over in my head. It goes like this:

Iamacowardwhitemanacowardwhitemanajamaicawhitecowardacowardjam—

The record never stops; it keeps on going. Most of the time it is barely audible, but it is always there and with no knob to turn it off—

Iamacowardwhitemanacowardwhitemanajamaicawhitecowardjamaicawhite mancowardcowardcowardwhitemanthat'swhatIamacowardjamaicawhite man—

Death has brought no relief—

Iamacowardwhitemanacowardwhitemanajamaicawhitecowardacoward jamaicacowardcowardwhitemanthat'swhatIamacowardwhitejamaica whitemanIamacowardwhitemanacowardwhitemanajamaicawhitecowarda cowardjamaicawhitecowardcowardcowardwhitemanthat'swhatIamacoward whitejamaicawhitemancowardwhitemanacowardwhitemanajamaicawhite cowardacowardjamaicacowardcowardwhitemanthat'swhatIamacowardwhite jamaicawhitemancowardmancowardwhitemanacowardwhitemanajamaica whitecowardacowardjamaicacowardcowardcowardwhitemanthat'swhatIama cowardwhitejamaicacoward—

That day, the little bastard just stood there watching me leave.

"Me wait for you but you never come back."

Norval studies the face in front of him.

"You are not the boy—"

"Is me. Is me the boy."

"Ugly as sin. And a liar too, you are."

Bob raises his hand as if to whip the whiteman's face; then thinks better of it; turns away and kicks the wall.

"The whiteman smell like pussy," a boy had said as Norval walked away. Bob remembers these words, sharp as bottle-glass now. "Pussyman!" the boy called when Norval couldn't hear no more.

"Is your faadah dat?" a girl asked. Bob felt ashamed and shook his head, "Nah," but still stood there watching, swallowing the bits of broken glass till they made a heap at the bottom of his stomach. He wanted to call the whiteman back, but didn't know what to call him. He was too fraid to call the whiteman "daddy."

There is one more spliff hidden in his hair. Bob lights it and draws in the smoke, holding it awhile before breathing out.

"Bloodclaat."

Norval preoccupies himself with picking feathers from his trousers. Up in the rafters, the congregation of brethren and sistren has grown quiet.

"You coulda put me on the bus and send me back to country." Bob inhales again. Then releases. "But check this; check the workings of Jah. The stone which the builder rejected has become Rastafari."

Mi chile, mi chile, mi chile, a woman outside bawls. Her wail sounds from pit-bottom pain-o-heart. Inside, bird droppings and dust fall from the rafters. And so the woman bawls, so the dark rain falls and so the veil is lifted from Bob's face till Norval, awakened, sees him—a boy with short-pants and riverbottom eyes, his back against a zinc fence: *Evening and there was yellow love bush everywhere, the lane lit up by a curious gold filtering from holes in the zinc fence. The boy's milk tooth had fallen out and he offered it, a sole possession, on his hand middle. Norval took the tooth and put it in his shirt pocket, then turned and walked away.*

"I promised you thruppence for the tooth," says Norval. "But what can this old fart do for you now?"

Bob outs the spliff and tucks the rest in his hair. Norval is as disappointing now as he was then. "Is late," he says. "You right. You miss your boat." He wants to forget it all, to go to sleep and wake up in the yet-to-come. It will be his last chance to find the gate. He rests his head on the satchel and closes his eyes, listens to the congregation stitching their drums.

"You cried that day, did you?" Norval whispers in the soon-dark.

The congregation hums.

"I wanted to call you back, but never know what to call you. I was too fraid too call a whiteman 'Daddy.'"

"But see, I'm here now."

"And is late. Two of us dead and lock-up inna Half Way Tree."

"I want to do something. There must be something a dead man can do. Nesta!"

"Bob. They call me Bob now."

"What can your dead father do?"

Outside a clamour of news beats the clock tower—chips of voices, streams of laughter. It sounds like a short-wave radio. Inside, the clock is warm and still. Bob raises himself up from the satchel and leans against the wall.

"Look me in my two eye. Tell me who you is. I always wanted to know who you really is."

Zion Gate VII; or, Revelation of Wisdom According to Jah Prophets

(3:25)

(For it is possible to journey to Zion through the vortex of your father's mottled eye. In this wheel you are taken through saltwater/ rotten tamarind/sorrowstones and gunshot/down a lane where a boy stands and waits for his daddy/all the way back to the stink of Columbus and the winds of contention/the sound of the sound of the heels of the unrighteous/corrupted and foolish they are/the song of a Taino woman on a stretch of lone beach/livity in her voice moving the water/Africa split open/a priestess catching the bullets of St. Babylon/war and rumour of rumour of/the hooves of destruction/botheration and heartlice/tribal bloodflies/the abomination of white salt/in your no cry eye—

Your father bli/nks/a yellow ring around his iris reeling to the quietness of a house on a hill with hibiscus and cassia flowers. You see him—your boy-faadah. Six years old. Holding a mouse. The salt of his tears. He must kill the mouse, mother said. He feeds it cheese, foolish boy. She gives him a bag to tie it up and throw it away. Coward, she says. He ties the knot, puts the bag in the piano, closes the lid, locks it and hides the key.

Something stinks in the piano. The piano stinks. There is stinking in the piano.

Nights the boy speaks to a piece of moon. It is still like the small white bones in the piano. I'm sorry, he says. I'm a coward, mother said so. *Beware, beware*, a lizard croaks. The moon sinks low behind the jackfruit tree as the boy closes his eyes and dreams of valour, his horse and sword scouring the land, saving mouse and rabbit and chick, every feeble, trembling thing. And you cry for this mawga, shame-face sleeping boy—your boy-faadah. You cry, for such pure of mind will soon come to naught/misshapen into wickedness/the wishapple turn rancid/but see him there now—the boy-sweetness of his mouth dreaming redemption/and, you forgive him. Unexpected eye-water/washes off/your heart.

Somewhere someone shakes a maraca. Spirit hands bear you high higher/Omeriah hums and

a woman wipes your face with her long-grey locs; holds you/yes-I/ like a chile/

"You found it"/she says,

"You found the gate.")

There is a peace that passes all higherstanding, a peace-mind not even a spliff can bring. The grey-hair woman has brought Bob's guitar; she offers it, arms stretched in the nowlight. Bob holds it careful as newborn baby. A small moth dances around the neck, flutters into the soundhole. Zion is Zion is Zion go the strings.

On the up-strum, a slave-boy with a noose around his throat appears in a corner of the clock tower. His feet are broad; tough-gong from running. There are 300-year tears in his eyes, and a word on the tip of his tongue.

"I want to play freedom song," says the boy.

"Is a place in the heart."

"I want to play it."

Bob hands him the guitar.

"I heard you play once," says the boy. "I danced to the music as I died and I heard the wail of a great multitude and a word filled me—"

The boy's noose is rotten; it falls from his neck, and he plays guitar through dreams of the fallen, and of bankrupt ships and muffled voices and lost language, and places of no hope and no light; across continents and centuries and back again; to an angel at a gate, and a girl reading a book; to Taino sister re-mixing the riddim; all the way to a far-off coast where a woman holds an ostrich egg and greets him on the shore.

"So long I've been waiting," she says.

DUB-SIDE CHANTING

Track 21.0: Bob Marley Returns
[Rewind]

All night Bob rests in the pretty grey-hair woman's arms. When he awakes, his head is on the rock at the bottom of the Dub Side. He is naked; his clothes neatly folded on the grass. He looks at his navel, his penis. There are still no lines on his palms, but at least the hands are his. His locs are gone; maybe they'll grow back. He puts on the redgreengold underwear, his pants and denim shirt; counts his toes and wriggles them.

H.I.M. is under the nutmeg tree, eyes closed and a smile on his face. He hears the Prophet's footsteps and blinks, awakened from dream.

The air is clean here; oxygen fills the Prophet's lungs and the effect is of a good lambsbread spliff. He breathes in deep drafts of it and feels every pore of his skin numbered.

"And so?" H.I.M. searches the Prophet's eyes.

Another green breadfruit falls on a roof in Babylon; and only then does Bob remember why he left.

AND WITH FULLTICIPATION,
THEY SAID

HERE-SO; HALF WAY TREE

Sixth Morning: Year of Yet-to-come
[in G Major]

Something is not right in Half Way Tree. There is a crowd gathered around the clock tower. The sky crazy-crazy with birds. The clouds are unusually low.

My mother get shot! My mother get shot! It's a young woman shouting and pushing her way through the crowd. A man tries to stop her, but the woman wheels free and screams a scream that comes from so deep it sends the whole of Half Way Tree to a halt.

Everyone recognizes the wail—the six generations of sufferation in the woman's voice. Its pitch holds all the mash-down parts of themselves– the holes in their hearts stuffed with dead children/rotten chicken-foot/the price of flour/Bata tight-shoes/cane trash and/wata lock-off and bloodclaat rage.

And this woman will not be held back. She parts the crowd, like Ras Moses parting the Red Sea. The people quiet; her mother on the ground, baptised in blood.

Mama bleeding; she bleeding. The blood too red. It red like Christmas poinsettia flowers. I want to call her name, but the word won't come.

"Mama!"

Leenah, her name is Leenah. I must not forget her name. She name after her great-grandmother, Murlina, who came to Jamaica from Cuba on a fishing boat; her locs smell of wood smoke and pimento and poinsettia blood. I must dwell in that smell; trod back through macca and woodland to a far-inside place. For a man came to me and said in a dream: *Open the Zion tin where Nana Vaughn loc keep*—the lozenges tin buried at the bottom of the yard in Mama's heart. *Open it*, he said. I must open it with the sound sistren of all our names.

"Mama!"

She get shot. My mother get shot. A hundred and forty-four locs baptised in blood. But the blood too red. The blood should not be as red as this.

"Mama?"

I am Anjahla Winnifred Morgan, half-angel daughter of Leenah, Rastawoman chile of Vaughn who built her house and lost it and built it again. *No weapon used against this house shall prosper.* Vaughn, daughter of Winnifred who lost her husband—Hector—to Millicent, and swept that corner clean and is the daughter-in-law of Murlina who crossed sea to a place of brackish water. Anjahla Vaughn, Leenah Winnifred, Vaughn Murlina, Winnifred Beryl, Murlina Shawn. If I call all our names it will open the Zion tin and Mama will hear; she will hear me.

"Mamaaaaa!"

THE PEOPLE

Babylon Is Fallen, Is Fallen

Seventeen minutes have passed and still no ambulance. The woman bleeds on the ground. The crowd is restless. The people look at each other; prayer and cuss under their breath. Someone puts a towel to soak the blood. A man picks up the woman's broom; it is carved with lizards, a long-neck priestess on top. Higher-standing, he begins to sweep. He sweeps a sweep of supplication. Bits of chewing gum, bird feather, tamarind pod. He sweeps. To strengthen the crowd/to hurry the ambulance/to remember the quiet/of his face in his shoes. He sweeps. And far-far on the roof of a carved-in-the-rock church in Ethiopia, another man stands and looks to the horizon. The roof of rock is wrought like a cross, but to the man it seems an X—a changing variable, a crossroad, a multiplication of sound. He takes his broom and sweeps the roof. *Jah live. Jah live.* Two men sweeping the far corners of the earth.

Nineteen minutes. Blood stains the concrete. The woman's daughter chants a strange language. The people trace Babylon, their cuss layered under the daughter's tuning. Wind blows open a girl's book; the leaves flap-flap, pale yellow-yellow. She holds up the book and lets the leaves fly. A madwoman across the street grips her knife, tastes a word on her tongue.

What kinda shitness. The policeman goes in his car; calls for back-up. The shot woman reminds him of his sister, her long dark toes in plastic slippers. He wishes now he did not shoot. The shot was meant for the man who broke into the clock tower. The man came out naked with a staff in his hand, chanting down Babylon. It was instinctual; he is so used to shooting. His gun—like an exten-sion of the body—went boom. He didn't see the woman coming from the other side of the tower. He didn't see her dark feet until it was too late. But he saw the man's eyes and the ancient spinning inside them—something not of this world. Maybe the spinning made the shot miss; the ground tilted at a strange angle as the earth skipped a beat. He should not have shot at all/he should not have shot at all/he should not have shot at all—

The people have had enough. Three men are shaking the car; the police revs the engine and pulls away from the sidewalk; locks the doors. Still they shake the car. He turns on the siren and revs the engine again. Where is back-up? The two in front jump on top of the hood and he pushes down the road with both of them still on it.

With the police gone, there is no one left for the people to turn on, and, anyway, they are tired of killing. That's when a young girl picks up the first stone. She runs across the street and flings it to the clock tower, smashing the face. More people follow, and soon stones and bottles are hurling from everywhere. A man throws a broken cell phone and the old woman next to him takes out her too-tight dentures, flings them, then bursts into roaring prayer Babylon! Traffic is piled up around the square; cars honk, women trace, dogs bark, youths cuss, men speak in tongues, the sky fills with unknown birds, a baby turns in womb, the vendors throw their worthless coins, and everywhere there is the riddim of an indignation more ancient and more to-come and more present than fiah.

THE YOUTH

Black Star Line Remix

But look here—an army of youth coming from the four directions and into the square. They come in hundreds, pour out from the seams of the island and down into Kingston. From Porus through May Pen; from Morant Bay through Bull Bay; from Annotto Bay down Junction; from Buff Bay through New Castle; from Trench Town and Rema and Waterhouse and Jones Town; with drum and guitar; bass and amp, bongo and trombone, dj and war maracas, they move decided as creatures in migration, answering a remembrance from the future. Their voices in fullticipation, they hum a bass so deep the island shudders; memem mem mem rememb ring/word, resting, for 300 years at the tip of the tongue—

Ash.

Ash.

Ashe.

Ashe/Ashe/Ashe/Ashe/Ashe/Ashe/Ashe!

Jah-Jah youth remem mem member them/I&I

They call gully water passage/routes without precinct/blood-ways/Jah-ways/higherground crossings/wake-up teachment/risen dread mighty/sound balmnation/bones I-rising/the new word written on the inside of a shoe.

zion-mind train/zion-mind train/zion-mind train/people get ready/zion-mind train/zion-mind train—

Ashe/Ashe/Ashe/Ashe/Ashe/Ashe/Ashe.

zion-mind train/zion-mind train/zion-mind train/people get ready/zion-mind train/zion-mind train—

Listen now. Listen. They are calling your name.

OUR MAD LADY OF HALF WAY TREE

Our Lady outside the clock stands still; looks up at the sky; counts the syllables in the air; cuts it with her knife. The ancestors have awakened, she says. Somebody has called them. The long-dead are stirring. Quick, she says. Sprinkle little rum. Hallelujah. Is it too late? Is it too late? *Dread of Zion, fall on me!* Redemption song. Redemption song. Jah ways are mysterious ways.

FROM BLOODFIAH, RECORD OF DREAMSLOST

Track 49.0: Glimmer

The ring in Red Ear's book is the ring the angel stole from Bob. And the ring the angel stole from Bob is the ring Prince Asfa Wossen gave to the prophet. The ring Prince Asfa Wossen gave to the prophet is the ring His Imperial Majesty wore on his right hand and the ring His Majesty wore on his right hand has seventy-seven copies, and copies of those copies from Ethiopia to London. Some people say His Majesty's ring contains bits of gold from the ring of Solomon. And some people say the ring of Solomon is the same one given to the Queen of Sheba—the ring Bayna-Lehkem presented to his father, to prove he was a true son.

The truth is, the secrets of Ethiopia are past finding out, inscrutable as a red velvet curtain at Axum or the laughter locked in Lucy's bones. According to the law of conservation of mass, matter can neither be created nor destroyed; however, it can be rearranged in space. Is this so? Maybe King Solomon's, like Les Vingt et Un, is hidden in a dream. Perhaps, it waits there. One night, someone's foot will slip in sleep and they will find it. They will put it on their finger and a page in Red Ear's book will be illuminated.

Ashe/Ashe/Ashe/Ashe/Ashe/Ashe/Ashe/Ashe/Ashe/Ashe/Ashe/
Ashe/Ashe/Ashe/Ashe/Ashe/Ashe/Ashe/Ashe/Ashe/Ashe/
Ashe/Ashe/AsheAshe/Ashe/Ashe/Ashe/Ashe/Ashe/Ashe/Ashe/
Ashe/Ashe/Ashe/Ashe/Ashe/Ashe/Ashe/Ashe/Ashe/Ashe/Ashe/
Ashe/Ashe/Ashe/Ashe/Ashe/Ashe/Ashe/Ashe/Ashe/Ashe/Ashe/
Ashe/Ashe/Ashe/Ashe/Ashe/Ashe/Ashe/Ashe/Ashe/Ashe/Ashe/
Ashe/Ashe/Ashe/Ashe/Ashe/Ashe/Ashe/Ashe/Ashe/Ashe/Ashe/
Ashe/Ashe/Ashe/Ashe/Ashe/Ashe/Ashe/Ashe/Ashe/Ashe/Ashe/
Ashe/Ashe/Ashe/Ashe/Ashe/Ashe/Ashe/Ashe/Ashe/Ashe/Ashe/
Ashe/Ashe/Ashe/Ashe/Ashe/Ashe/Ashe/Ashe/Ashe/Ashe/Ashe/
Ashe/Ashe/Ashe/Ashe/Ashe/Ashe/Ashe/Ashe/Ashe/Ashe/Ashe/
Ashe/Ashe/Ashe/Ashe/Ashe/Ashe/Ashe/Ashe/Ashe/Ashe/Ashe/
Ashe/Ashe/Ashe/Ashe/Ashe/Ashe/Ashe/Ashe/Ashe/Ashe/Ashe/
Ashe/Ashe/Ashe/Ashe/Ashe/Ashe/Ashe/Ashe/Ashe/Ashe/Ashe/
Ashe/Ashe/Ashe/Ashe/Ashe/Ashe/Ashe/Ashe/Ashe/Ashe/Ashe/
Ashe/Ashe/Ashe/Ashe/Ashe/Ashe/Ashe/Ashe/Ashe/Ashe/Ashe/
Ashe/Ashe/Ashe/Ashe/Ashe/Ashe/Ashe/Ashe/Ashe/Ashe/Ashe/
Ashe/Ashe/Ashe/Ashe/Ashe/Ashe/Ashe/Ashe/Ashe/Ashe/Ashe/
Ashe/Ashe/Ashe/Ashe/Ashe/Ashe/Ashe/Ashe/Ashe/Ashe/Ashe/
Ashe/Ashe/Ashe/Ashe/Ashe/Ashe/Ashe/Ashe/Ashe/Ashe/Ashe/
Ashe/Ashe/Ashe/Ashe/Ashe/Ashe/Ashe/Ashe/Ashe/Ashe/Ashe/
Ashe/Ashe/Ashe/Ashe/Ashe/Ashe/Ashe/Ashe/Ashe/Ashe/Ashe/
Ashe/Ashe/Ashe/Ashe/Ashe/Ashe/Ashe/Ashe/Ashe/Ashe/Ashe/
Ashe/Ashe/Ashe/Ashe/Ashe/Ashe/Ashe/Ashe/Ashe/Ashe/Ashe/
Ashe/Ashe/Ashe/Ashe/Ashe/Ashe/Ashe/Ashe/Ashe/Ashe/Ashe/
Ashe/Ashe/Ashe/Ashe/Ashe/Ashe/Ashe/Ashe/Ashe/Ashe/Ashe/
Ashe/Ashe/Ashe/Ashe/Ashe/Ashe/Ashe/Ashe/Ashe/Ashe/Ashe/
Ashe/Ashe/Ashe/Ashe/Ashe/Ashe/Ashe/Ashe/Ashe/Ashe/Ashe/
Ashe/Ashe/Ashe/Ashe/Ashe/Ashe/Ashe/Ashe/Ashe/Ashe/Ashe/
Ashe/Ashe/Ashe/Ashe/Ashe/Ashe/Ashe/Ashe/Ashe/Ashe/Ashe/
Ashe/Ashe/Ashe/Ashe/Ashe/Ashe/Ashe/Ashe/Ashe/Ashe/Ashe/
Ashe/Ashe/Ashe/Ashe/Ashe/Ashe/Ashe/Ashe/Ashe/Ashe/Ashe/
Ashe/Ashe/Ashe/Ashe/Ashe/Ashe/Ashe/Ashe/Ashe/Ashe/Ashe/
Ashe/Ashe/Ashe/Ashe/Ashe/Ashe/Ashe/Ashe/Ashe/Ashe/Ashe/
Ashe/Ashe/Ashe/Ashe/Ashe/Ashe/Ashe/Ashe/Ashe/Ashe/Ashe/

HELLSHIRE

A madman runs naked down Hagley Park Road. No one pays him much attention; the people are used to the insane. We all have a mad part of ourselves, no true? A part that wants to run naked, like this man with the brass Africas at his ears that go ting&ting. His legs are long and powerful. Maybe he is the bronze statue of the slave at Emancipation Park cut lose and looking for his woman. Maybe he is God's rebel bird. He runs and runs, calling a woman's name and reciting a strange *poesie*. At Hellshire Beach the salt waves whip him and he rolls in the sand and the sand covers his nakedness. People call him the Fall-down of Hellshire. He is what mountains look like when they move—

Ashe/Ashe/Ashe/Ashe/Ashe/Ashe/Ashe/Ashe/Ashe/Ashe/Ashe/
Ashe/Ashe/Ashe/Ashe/Ashe/Ashe/Ashe/Ashe/Ashe/Ashe/Ashe/
Ashe/Ashe/Ashe/Ashe/Ashe/Ashe/Ashe/Ashe/Ashe/Ashe/Ashe/
Ashe/Ashe/Ashe/Ashe/Ashe/Ashe/Ashe/Ashe/Ashe/Ashe/Ashe/
Ashe/Ashe/Ashe/Ashe/Ashe/Ashe/Ashe/Ashe/Ashe/Ashe/Ashe/
Ashe/Ashe/Ashe/Ashe/Ashe/Ashe/Ashe/Ashe/Ashe/Ashe/Ashe/
Ashe/Ashe/Ashe/Ashe/Ashe/Ashe/Ashe/Ashe/Ashe/Ashe/Ashe/
Ashe/Ashe/Ashe/Ashe/Ashe/Ashe/Ashe/Ashe/Ashe/Ashe/Ashe/
Ashe/Ashe/Ashe/Ashe/Ashe/Ashe/Ashe/Ashe/Ashe/Ashe/Ashe/
Ashe/Ashe/Ashe/Ashe/Ashe/Ashe/Ashe/Ashe/Ashe/Ashe/Ashe/
Ashe/Ashe/Ashe/Ashe/Ashe/Ashe/Ashe/Ashe/Ashe/Ashe/Ashe/
Ashe/Ashe/Ashe/Ashe/Ashe/Ashe/Ashe/Ashe/Ashe/Ashe/Ashe/
Ashe/Ashe/Ashe/Ashe/Ashe/Ashe/Ashe/Ashe/Ashe/Ashe/Ashe/
Ashe/Ashe/Ashe/Ashe/Ashe/Ashe/Ashe/Ashe/Ashe/Ashe/Ashe/
Ashe/Ashe/Ashe/Ashe/Ashe/Ashe/Ashe/Ashe/Ashe/Ashe/Ashe/
Ashe/Ashe/Ashe/Ashe/Ashe/Ashe/Ashe/Ashe/Ashe/Ashe/Ashe/
Ashe/Ashe/Ashe/Ashe/Ashe/Ashe/Ashe/Ashe/Ashe/Ashe/Ashe/
Ashe/Ashe/Ashe/Ashe/Ashe/Ashe/Ashe/Ashe/Ashe/Ashe/Ashe/
Ashe/Ashe/Ashe/Ashe/Ashe/Ashe/Ashe/Ashe/Ashe/Ashe/Ashe/
Ashe/Ashe/Ashe/Ashe/Ashe/Ashe/Ashe/Ashe/Ashe/Ashe/Ashe/
Ashe/Ashe/Ashe/Ashe/Ashe/Ashe/Ashe/Ashe/Ashe/Ashe/Ashe/
Ashe/Ashe/Ashe/Ashe/Ashe/Ashe/Ashe/Ashe/Ashe/Ashe/Ashe/
Ashe/Ashe/Ashe/Ashe/Ashe/Ashe/Ashe/Ashe/Ashe/Ashe/Ashe/
Ashe/Ashe/Ashe/Ashe/Ashe/Ashe/Ashe/Ashe/Ashe/Ashe/Ashe/
Ashe/Ashe/Ashe/Ashe/Ashe/Ashe/Ashe/Ashe/Ashe/Ashe/Ashe/
Ashe/Ashe/Ashe/Ashe/Ashe/Ashe/Ashe/Ashe/Ashe/Ashe/Ashe/
Ashe/Ashe/Ashe/Ashe/Ashe/Ashe/Ashe/Ashe/Ashe/Ashe/Ashe/
Ashe/Ashe/Ashe/Ashe/Ashe/Ashe/Ashe/Ashe/Ashe/Ashe/Ashe/
Ashe/Ashe/Ashe/Ashe/Ashe/Ashe/Ashe/Ashe/Ashe/Ashe/Ashe/
Ashe/Ashe/Ashe/Ashe/Ashe/Ashe/Ashe/Ashe/Ashe/Ashe/Ashe/
Ashe/Ashe/Ashe/Ashe/Ashe/Ashe/Ashe/Ashe/Ashe/Ashe/Ashe/
Ashe/Ashe/Ashe/Ashe/Ashe/Ashe/Ashe/Ashe/Ashe/Ashe/Ashe/
Ashe/Ashe/Ashe/Ashe/Ashe/Ashe/Ashe/Ashe/Ashe/Ashe/Ashe/
Ashe/Ashe/Ashe/Ashe/Ashe/Ashe/Ashe/Ashe/Ashe/Ashe/Ashe/

DUB-SIDE CHANTING

On the Far Side of I&I

The highly concentrated oxygen on the mountain-top comes from the exhalation of the nutmeg trees. It is nutmeg season and the fruits are bursting open, the dark seeds covered with red thread. H.I.M. and the Prophet walk amid the trees, collecting fruit. The seeds absorb leftover badmindedness, replace Babylon mind with Zion mind.

"I&I gave the ring to a dawta reading a book," Bob says.

H.I.M. sets his sack down before replying; looks his son in the eyes.

"It will be safe there. Books have a way of preserving things."

And this time, the Prophet knows that the work is not for him alone; others will come after. He breathes in, then out. He will dwell in this nyahmbic place, a dub-side warrior/holding communion with H.I.M. and the ancestors/visiting the visions of the youth and the dreams of the old ones/urging the people on—Wake up! Wake up! Until one day when the earth tilts just-so/he will be called back again. But for now, they fill their sacks, and the nutmeg trees exhale—

Ashe/Ashe/Ashe/Ashe/Ashe/Ashe/Ashe/Ashe/Ashe/Ashe/Ashe/
Ashe/Ashe/Ashe/Ashe/Ashe/Ashe/Ashe/Ashe/Ashe/Ashe/Ashe/
Ashe/Ashe/Ashe/Ashe/Ashe/Ashe/Ashe/Ashe/Ashe/Ashe/Ashe/
Ashe/Ashe/Ashe/Ashe/Ashe/Ashe/Ashe/Ashe/Ashe/Ashe/Ashe/
Ashe/Ashe/Ashe/Ashe/Ashe/Ashe/Ashe/Ashe/Ashe/Ashe/Ashe/
Ashe/Ashe/Ashe/Ashe/Ashe/Ashe/Ashe/Ashe/Ashe/Ashe/Ashe/
Ashe/Ashe/Ashe/Ashe/Ashe/Ashe/Ashe/Ashe/Ashe/Ashe/Ashe/
Ashe/Ashe/Ashe/Ashe/Ashe/Ashe/Ashe/Ashe/Ashe/Ashe/Ashe/
Ashe/Ashe/Ashe/Ashe/Ashe/Ashe/Ashe/Ashe/Ashe/Ashe/Ashe/
Ashe/Ashe/Ashe/Ashe/Ashe/Ashe/Ashe/Ashe/Ashe/Ashe/Ashe/
Ashe/Ashe/Ashe/Ashe/Ashe/Ashe/Ashe/Ashe/Ashe/Ashe/Ashe/
Ashe/Ashe/Ashe/Ashe/Ashe/Ashe/Ashe/Ashe/Ashe/Ashe/Ashe/
Ashe/Ashe/Ashe/Ashe/Ashe/Ashe/Ashe/Ashe/Ashe/Ashe/Ashe/
Ashe/Ashe/Ashe/Ashe/Ashe/Ashe/Ashe/Ashe/Ashe/Ashe/Ashe/
Ashe/Ashe/Ashe/Ashe/Ashe/Ashe/Ashe/Ashe/Ashe/Ashe/Ashe/
Ashe/Ashe/Ashe/Ashe/Ashe/Ashe/Ashe/Ashe/Ashe/Ashe/Ashe/
Ashe/Ashe/Ashe/Ashe/Ashe/Ashe/Ashe/Ashe/Ashe/Ashe/Ashe/
Ashe/Ashe/Ashe/Ashe/Ashe/Ashe/Ashe/Ashe/Ashe/Ashe/Ashe/
Ashe/Ashe/Ashe/Ashe/Ashe/Ashe/Ashe/Ashe/Ashe/Ashe/Ashe/
Ashe/Ashe/Ashe/Ashe/Ashe/Ashe/Ashe/Ashe/Ashe/Ashe/Ashe/
Ashe/Ashe/Ashe/Ashe/Ashe/Ashe/Ashe/Ashe/Ashe/Ashe/Ashe/
Ashe/Ashe/Ashe/Ashe/Ashe/Ashe/Ashe/Ashe/Ashe/Ashe/Ashe/
Ashe/Ashe/Ashe/Ashe/Ashe/Ashe/Ashe/Ashe/Ashe/Ashe/Ashe/
Ashe/Ashe/Ashe/Ashe/Ashe/Ashe/Ashe/Ashe/Ashe/Ashe/Ashe/
Ashe/Ashe/Ashe/Ashe/Ashe/Ashe/Ashe/Ashe/Ashe/Ashe/Ashe/
Ashe/Ashe/Ashe/Ashe/Ashe/Ashe/Ashe/Ashe/Ashe/Ashe/Ashe/
Ashe/Ashe/Ashe/Ashe/Ashe/Ashe/Ashe/Ashe/Ashe/Ashe/Ashe/
Ashe/Ashe/Ashe/Ashe/Ashe/Ashe/Ashe/Ashe/Ashe/Ashe/Ashe/
Ashe/Ashe/Ashe/Ashe/Ashe/Ashe/Ashe/Ashe/Ashe/Ashe/Ashe/
Ashe/Ashe/Ashe/Ashe/Ashe/Ashe/Ashe/Ashe/Ashe/Ashe/Ashe/
Ashe/Ashe/Ashe/Ashe/Ashe/Ashe/Ashe/Ashe/Ashe/Ashe/Ashe/
Ashe/Ashe/Ashe/Ashe/Ashe/Ashe/Ashe/Ashe/Ashe/Ashe/Ashe/
Ashe/Ashe/Ashe/Ashe/Ashe/Ashe/Ashe/Ashe/Ashe/Ashe/Ashe/
Ashe/Ashe/Ashe/Ashe/Ashe/Ashe/Ashe/Ashe/Ashe/Ashe/Ashe/

HERE-SO; HALF WAY TREE
LEENAH

Of Lioness Uprising; or, The Ship of Zion

The two lions in my dream have changed. Their manes are gone, and the tilt of their head is different. I&I stand between them and they roar, for this is the last time I will stand in this place. The roar shakes the last of my little eggs; I feel blood between my legs. Then it dawns on me—I know why their manes are gone. They are female. A woman from Burkina Faso told me why she shaved her head. To keep her focused, she said. Her hair picked up too much energy, she said. I&I know about this. I feel the ancestors tugging at my locs; I feel storms when they are way out at sea. I wrap my locs to contain this power, to hold such knowing and not be distracted. The lions in my dream are queens in control of their knowing. I she-magine them, Rasta sistahs, their head wrapped with Zion cloth. They know what they know and that knowing grounds them, sustains them.

The lions shift their gaze to the horizon. Someone is coming; I look back and it is Anjahla, running, her thin arms protruding the way they do; her face wet with tears. She stops, breathless, at the bottom of the step, for the lions will not let her any further. She holds up a lozenges tin—with Vaughn's loc curled inside. I recognize the loc even from here. And on the side of the tin, my true name—Zion. I am that far-I place.

But look at my Anjahla. When she was a baby her tears smelled like rose water. Now they smell like strong kananga. Lioness arrive. Behind her are the voices of one thousand youth, a mighty chanting that troubles the ground. The ancestors are awake and the youth have been summoned. Is it too late? Is it too late for this bass-yard nation?

All of this as the rain begins to fall and my red blood seeps in cracks in the concrete, and my one-daughter, Anjahla, calls me— Mama! And, I&I *hear* her. I hear my Anjahla.

NYAHBINGHI

SISTAFARI CHANTING
[SIS. DAWN, WILLA & MAUVA]

Track 33.0: How to Trace the Palm of an Island

Map every river, every hill and every woodland, marking the neva-catch-mi foot-trails of maroons.

Trace over that with the routes of doctor birds and swallowtails, libating old bones and burial grounds with rum.

With your ear to the ground, wait for the echo of wild hogs in labour, 100-year whooping cough, barking dogs, the Middle "C" of a Steinway (ordered special from London), a lamentation of waves/slap against shore, the click of a muzzle over a young boy's mouth.

Follow the curve of this song, and listen/for where it dubs over with seeds in a calabash, tongues of fire, black birds in an orange poinciana. Mark where the birds leave feathers, and whether the feathers point up hill or down.

Map the ground—coast to coast—for red clay or dark; note the remembrance of blood, broken water, thrown-away seed.

Layer over that the cuss-cuss of children coming home from school, the pathways of gunshots, the lethal yellowing of trees.

Know what it means if the rain over Emancipation Park is light or hard.

Know what it means if a shaft of red light shines through the glass star on the prophet's tomb.

Know what it means if roots at Half Way Tree grow overground.

And know what it means if the bassline dips: the fowls lay rebel eggs, and the people rhaatid eat them. For/

such fiah awakens ancestors/
translates Jahrithmetic/
ignites equations/
grows back lizard tails seven times seven/

Know-oh what it means if the island flings herself to the sea—for the sea is our mother and a mother covers her child's nakedness with raiment,
   and chanting zion tings.

(And the ancestor says, "Speak/this. Speak it down in the book.")
Ashe.

*Ashe: (Ah-shey) "the power to make things happen"/"the power to create change"/"and so it is." (Yoruba/W. Africa)

APPENDIX I: BACKSTAGE PASS

In my father's house are many mansions—John, 14:2

What the maidservant saw

Translation of Meharene's note to Haile Selassie I
(1 of 3 found by a Dergue soldier in the floorboards of the Jubilee
Palace. Original written in Amharic on unlined paper.)

For the beads Côte d'Ivoire, thank you.

Your new pyjamas are under our blue pillow.
—Meharene

*

Translation of lines 34–35 of Rimbaud's Vingt et Un
(as found in an archive of Selassie's dream.)

Nutmeg trees are male and female. Didn't they tell you?
Rouge/rouge, rouge, the sky when they bleed.
                                                                —Arthur Rimbaud

*

Excerpt from interview with Haile Selassie I
*Sunday, June 24, 1973 by Oriana Fallaci/*Chicago Tribune

Fallaci: Your Majesty, I would like you to tell me something about yourself. Tell me were you ever a disobedient youth? But maybe I ought to ask you first whether you have ever had time to be young, Your Majesty?

Selassie: We don't understand that question. What kind of question is that? It is obvious that We have been young. We weren't born old! We have been a child, a boy, a youth, an adult, and finally an old man. Like everyone else. Our Lord the Creator made us like eveyone else.

*

From the Lion's Mouth
My Life and Ethiopia's Progress *(1976)*

A house built on granite and strong foundations, not even the on-slaught of pouring rain, gushing torrents and strong winds will be able to pull down. Some people have written the story of my life representing as truth what in fact derives from ignorance, error or envy; but they cannot shake the truth from its place, even if they attempt to make others believe it.

Remember this ...

His Imperial Majesty, the Lion of Judah, greets his next-of-kin
Much Respect

APPENDIX II: STUDIO PASS

Half Way Tree; circa 1899. Revolution begins in a woman's basket. Note, too, the child and her mother (left), waiting for the doors of York Pharmacy to open.

Half Way Tree church and courthouse, circa 1890. Cotton Tree to the far left. See? There are two women sitting underneath. A man walks down the road; wonders at the far far-away vibration of bass—coming from over one hundred years in the future.

Look good. Here the women are—under the spot where a boy's feet danced.

And the man. Here he is—walking towards the strange music—

and here, walking towards you, bass riddim calling roots underground.

I'm a rebel; let them talk.
      —RNM

                              run it/for the people—

GIVING THANKS

to Barbara Epler, Mieke Chew and everyone at New Directions for running the riddim; to Peepal Tree for their support; to the National Endowment for the Arts; for the Book Semester Grant from CU English; to the musicians and historians who ignited my imagination; to Laurent and Avani for always believing in me, no matter what; to my supportive family; to Indira for cheering me on; to Cecilia for helping me put my voice out there; to Eliot for catching the vision; to Jamaica—dread and powerful; to the Most High Zion; to the great silk cotton of Half Way Tree; and for the marvellous equations of our ancestors.

Ashe.

Versions of some of the chapters in this book appeared in *The Edinburgh Review* (2008) and *Caribbean Erotic: Poetry, Prose and Essays* (2010)

New Directions Paperbooks — a partial listing

Javier Marías, Your Face Tomorrow (3 volumes)
Harry Mathews, The Solitary Twin
Bernadette Mayer, Works & Days
Carson McCullers, The Member of the Wedding
Thomas Merton, New Seeds of Contemplation
   The Way of Chuang Tzu
Henri Michaux, A Barbarian in Asia
Dunya Mikhail, The Beekeeper
Henry Miller, The Colossus of Maroussi
   Big Sur & The Oranges of Hieronymus Bosch
Yukio Mishima, Confessions of a Mask
   Death in Midsummer
Eugenio Montale, Selected Poems*
Vladimir Nabokov, Laughter in the Dark
   Nikolai Gogol
   The Real Life of Sebastian Knight
Raduan Nassar, A Cup of Rage
Pablo Neruda, The Captain's Verses*
   Love Poems*
   Residence on
Charles Olson, Selected Writings
George Oppen, New Collected Poems
Wilfred Owen, Collected Poems
Michael Palmer, The Laughter of the Sphinx
Nicanor Parra, Antipoems*
Boris Pasternak, Safe Conduct
Kenneth Patchen
   Memoirs of a Shy Pornographer
Octavio Paz, Poems of Octavio Paz
Victor Pelevin, Omon Ra
Alejandra Pizarnik
   Extracting the Stone of Madness
Ezra Pound, The Cantos
   New Selected Poems and Translations
Raymond Queneau, Exercises in Style
Qian Zhongshu, Fortress Besieged
Raja Rao, Kanthapura
Herbert Read, The Green Child
Kenneth Rexroth, Selected Poems
Keith Ridgway, Hawthorn & Child
Rainer Maria Rilke
   Poems from the Book of Hours
Arthur Rimbaud, Illuminations*
   A Season in Hell and The Drunken Boat*
Guillermo Rosales, The Halfway House
Evelio Rosero, The Armies
Fran Ross, Oreo
Joseph Roth, The Emperor's Tomb
   The Hotel Years

Raymond Roussel, Locus Solus
Ihara Saikaku, The Life of an Amorous Woman
Nathalie Sarraute, Tropisms
Jean-Paul Sartre, Nausea
   The Wall
Delmore Schwartz
   In Dreams Begin Responsibilities
Hasan Shah, The Dancing Girl
W. G. Sebald, The Emigrants
   The Rings of Saturn
   Vertigo
Stevie Smith, Best Poems
Gary Snyder, Turtle Island
Muriel Spark, The Driver's Seat
   The Girls of Slender Means
   Memento Mori
Reiner Stach, Is That Kafka?
Antonio Tabucchi, Pereira Maintains
Junichiro Tanizaki, A Cat, a Man & Two Wome
Yoko Tawada, The Emissary
   Memoirs of a Polar Bear
Dylan Thomas, A Child's Christmas in Wales
   Collected Poems
Uwe Timm, The Invention of Curried Sausage
Tomas Tranströmer
   The Great Enigma: New Collected Poems
Leonid Tsypkin, Summer in Baden-Baden
Tu Fu, Selected Poems
Frederic Tuten, The Adventures of Mao
Regina Ullmann, The Country Road
Paul Valéry, Selected Writings
Enrique Vila-Matas, Bartleby & Co.
   Vampire in Love
Elio Vittorini, Conversations in Sicily
Rosmarie Waldrop, Gap Gardening
Robert Walser, The Assistant
   Microscripts
   The Tanners
Eliot Weinberger, The Ghosts of Birds
Nathanael West, The Day of the Locust
   Miss Lonelyhearts
Tennessee Williams, Cat on a Hot Tin Roof
   The Glass Menagerie
   A Streetcar Named Desire
William Carlos Williams, Selected Poems
   Spring and All
Mushtaq Ahmed Yousufi, Mirages of the Min
Louis Zukofsky, "A"
   Anew

*BILINGUAL EDITION

For a complete listing, request a free catalog from New Directions, 80 8th Avenue, New York, NY 10011 or visit us online at ndbooks.com